S0-ARI-301

A Promise Kept

A Novel

By

Billy Doniel

Salt Island Publications

Salt Island Publications
P.O. Box 2823
Tybee Island, Georgia 31328

Copyright © 2000 by Salt Island Publications,
a division of Salt Island Incorporated
All rights reserved
With the exception of excerpts from ancient scripture, no part of this publication may be repro-
duced, stored in, or introduced into a
retrieval system, or transmitted in any form, or by
any means without prior permission
of the copyright owner

Original artwork and cover design
by Linda Lindeborg

PUBLISHER'S NOTE
This novel is a work of fiction. The author has,
however, used the actual names of some real
people in fictitious ways by permission.
Otherwise, names, characters, places, and inci-
dents are either a product of the author's imagination or are used fictitiously.
Any resemblance to actual persons, living or dead,
events, or locales is entirely coincidental.

ISBN: 0-9654922-0-6
Library of Congress Catalog Card Number: 96-69803

Printed in the United States Of America

ACKNOWLEDGMENTS

I would like to thank the following people for their support and encouragement:

K.B., who wishes to remain anonymous, for helping with the first edit of this book.

Jerry Sapp, for technical information regarding decompression and navigation.

Rik Lindeborg for his modeling skills.

My grandfather, W.C. Bateman Sr., who taught me to persevere and to reach for the stars.

And most of all, I want to thank my wife, Veronica, for her tireless work, her hours of study and research, her dedication, and her faith. Without her, this novel would still be only a dream. Thank you, Veronica, for believing in me. I love you.

Billy Doniel

This work is dedicated to the memory of

Teresa Yarbrough

Chapter I

E arly Friday morning Sam Lewis awoke to screeching sea gulls. Squabbling and prancing below his window, they awaited the turning tide. Then they could seek out mindless crustaceans hidden beneath the sand. The little creatures felt safety in their crystalline refuge. They were wrong, wrong from the beginning.

Sam begrudgingly opened one eye and scanned the familiar surroundings. He felt contempt for the shrill, piercing cries that brought him back from *his* refuge, from his dreams.

"Garbage cans with wings," grunted Sam as he lifted himself to a sitting position, in stages, wincing at each stage. He twisted to the edge of the bed, put his feet on the floor, and carefully surveyed his room. He was alone; that was good. His wallet was on the night stand; that was good too. On more than one occasion Sam awoke in strange places lying next to women whose names didn't readily come to mind. But that was all behind him.

Sam rose to his feet and stretched through the loss of memory from the night before. He ambled to the bathroom, drew the shower curtain, turned on the faucet and adjusted the spray. He unwrapped a fresh bar of deodorant soap, smelled the fragrance, and stepped into the shower.

1

The hot water felt good to Sam as it cascaded over his head and down his body. He stood a long time while the hydra-needles jabbed his face. He ran his fingers through his shoulder-length, brown hair, then rubbed his neatly trimmed beard and mustache, rinsing out the soap.

Feeling like a new man, he came out of the shower and dried off. He brushed his teeth and went back to his bedroom. He stood in front of the mirror, pulled his hair into a pony tail, and slipped a Goody Pony Elastic around the wet lock. The lines on his face were growing deeper but he looked younger than his forty years.

Sam slid back the louvered bi-fold closet doors. Bent coat hangers, un-ironed shirts and shorts, tennis shoes, flip flops, and an old pair of work boots were strewn about the closet. There were sweatshirts, tank tops, and things foreign even to Sam.

His dive gear was another matter. His buoyancy control vest was neatly folded and packed inside his canvas duffel bag. Attached to his vest was a stainless steel dagger and a rubber bullet holder housing twelve .357 magnum cartridges. His flippers, weight belt, regulator, and mask were carefully packed beside the vest.

Sam's steel air tank sat upright in the corner of the closet. Beside it stood his teakwood spear gun with a deadly power head screwed to the shaft. His spear gun was his favorite possession. It helped him feed himself and on more than one occasion it had saved his life.

He chose a pair of gray jogging pants, tennis shoes, and a turquoise sweatshirt emblazoned with, "I survived the Shipwreck...DeSoto Beach Motel...Tybee Island, Georgia." The cabana was small but nice. There was a kitchenette Sam rarely used, but he could cook when he felt like it. Beside the stove was a small refrigerator where he kept an ample supply of Coke and ice cubes to mix with his Canadian whiskey, O.F.C.

Sam moved back to the night stand, slid on his sun glasses, and reached for a pack of generic menthol cigarettes lying next to a full ash tray. He lit the menthol, inhaled, and awaited the rumbling cough. It came. Through his coughing Sam blurted, "I gotta quit these damn things...one day."

His attention returned to the gulls. On his way to the vertical, crank-out glass, Sam grabbed a handful of pizza ribs from an open box on the credenza. He opened the window and started tossing the pieces of pizza crust out.

The gulls went insane. It entertained Sam to watch the birds attack the crust. He threw the remaining ribs into the crowd and they went crazy again, pecking, flapping their wings, and playing beak tug-of-war with the crust.

"Garbage cans with wings," Sam groaned as he cranked the window closed.

2

The morning sun felt good on Sam's face as he latched the door behind him. He stood a moment enjoying the view. It was warm for January. Memories of the cold were swept away by gentle breezes wafting in off the Atlantic. Those sensitive winds were given birth in places Sam visited when he wore his diving suit a lot more than he had been wearing it lately. He snuffed his cigarette in a standing sand-filled ash tray and walked across the mosaic prom- enade that separated the cabana from the main building of the DeSoto Beach Motel.

He walked up the stout, wooden steps leading to the open air tiki bar which was empty. That was fine with Sam. He just wanted to sit in his worm wood chair, listen to the ocean, and watch his day come into existence. It had been nearly a year since that first morning when he sat pondering the sea and wondering at the fate that brought him there. Since then, every morning began the same.

Sam thought of Islamorada Key, Florida, and the miles ahead of him. Deciding to leave had been no task. He'd been thinking about it ever since he began his sabbatical. He employed the Benjamin Franklin method of decision making and put it down in black and white. He listed all the reasons to stay, then listed all the reasons to go.

The Florida Keys were beautiful and the weather was nearly always warm. This time tomorrow he'd be taking a dip in Florida Bay and he wouldn't even need his wet suit. When the big hurricane ripped through south Florida, it left an abundance of reconstruction to be done in its wake and, as a Master plumber, he'd have no difficulty getting his share. He hadn't been there in years, that's where he'd always wanted to be, and the list went on and on. It all seemed logical and the figures didn't lie.

In Islamorada he could start all over again. But this time he'd make good on his promise and never let anyone get too close to him. He'd stay to himself and not get involved. He'd work a little, dive a little, and have a happy, balanced life. He'd come home in the evenings, pour himself an O.F.C. and Coke, sit in his porch swing, and watch the sun go down. But how could he just disappear and pretend nothing ever happened?

His biggest reason to leave was his only reason not to. That made a lot of sense, Sam thought cynically. It made about as much sense as everything else had been making lately. The only thing that made more sense was not thinking about it at all. But that didn't work. It wouldn't take much to change his mind. He didn't know what it would take to change hers. The night before he gave up trying.

A gentle but labored smile crossed his lips when he heard, "G'day mate...here's the usual."

Sam removed his sunglasses as Brittany's shadow came between him and the morning sun. Brit, as Sam always called her, was a statuesque Australian with natural blonde hair and a tropical tan. She had ocean-green eyes and perfect teeth.

"I didn't expect to see you this morning. Not after last night anyway," Sam said, reaching for another cigarette.

Brit leaned over and placed his Bloody Mary on the worm wood table next to his chair. She straightened up to her nearly six foot height, wiped her brow, and looked out over the ocean.

The shrimping season had been extended through the end of the month because mild weather had produced an abundance of shrimp. A trawler groaned. Its engine strained to propel the boat while the wench dragged the captive bounty closer to the stern. Legions of gulls screamed as they dove after the lucky morsels who'd somehow escaped the nets.

"There'll be birds for you to grumble about down there too, you know," Brit said, delicately touching his temple.

Sam eyed her a moment, like he eyed her every morning, then said, "Uh huh."

"I suppose you'll be leaving straight away."

"Yep."

"You know I love you, Sam'o," she said.

Sam picked up his Bloody Mary, stirred the ice, then tasted the pungent cocktail. He licked his upper lip, took another swallow, and set the drink back down.

"All men *were not* created equal, Brit...I *am not* Jimmy Nesbit."

"I know," Brit said, reaching into her apron for a tissue. "I know you're nothing like he was." She turned away from Sam and wiped her eyes.

"You're too much alive to let someone control you...especially from the grave," said Sam.

"You're a very complicated man, Sam

Lewis."

"No I'm not. I'm a very simple man. I'm a simple man and I know what I want."

"Don't go," her voice trembled, her thoughts were racing along.

"God knows, Brit. If it weren't for you, I'd never have known love. But you are tearing my heart out. I'll ask you once more. Will you marry me?" Sam came to his feet and faced her directly.

Brit's lip quivered and her eyes filled with tears as she searched for the answer.

"I...I can't tell you...Oh Sam'o, for God's sake. Please! Please give me just a little more time." Her tears began to fall.

"I've given you time. You know I'll never hurt you, Brit. I want to give you my life. Please, won't you just say yes?"

After moments of silence, Sam turned and started back toward the cabana. Brit didn't follow him. She only listened to the sound of his footsteps fading as he walked away.

3

When Sam and Brit first met, their mutual attraction was sudden and strong. They would have become lovers but circumstances got in the way. That was back in July when she said she'd only been with one man and that one left her a taste as bitter as bile. As time went by, Sam came to understand.

Brit was raised an only child in the sub-tropical paradise of Brisbane, in the state of Queensland, Australia. Her house was a traditional Queenslander built of hardwood with a high-pitched roof wrought of galvanized, corrugated iron. The stately home stood in one of Brisbane's beautiful suburban gardens overlooking the cool waters of Kodak Beach lagoon. The wide verandah provided shade for lush birdnest ferns, and sanctuary for wild lorikeets, king parrots, and brilliantly plumaged bowerbirds that came to feed and visit her there.

As Brit grew, so did her interest in the sea and the wonder of the Great Barrier Reef. With encouragement from her father, she became an accomplished scuba diver. Underwater photography was her first passion and her home was adorned with dazzling color prints that attested to her skill with a camera.

When she was eighteen, Brit began studying Oceanography at the University of Queensland. Although the University wasn't far, a desire to make her own way prompted her move to the dormitory. She took a part-time position at the Botanical Gardens to supplement the living allowance provided by her father. She was glad to get the money, but she delighted in the new-found feeling of independence her job gave her.

Brit's father, Wilton Hayes, was a man of integrity. His wife died giving birth to Brit. He raised the child with a loving heart, placing her well-being above his own. He taught her dignity, humility and accountability. He instilled in her the virtues of chastity, monogamy and commitment.

Brit believed intimacy was a sacred trust, reserved for the man with whom she would share her life, until death. She was twenty years old when she told Jimmy Nesbit she wasn't ready to make that commitment. Jimmy was twenty-one and accustomed to having his way.

Orphaned at nineteen, Jimmy received a substantial inheritance when his father, who, out of sheer frustration over Mrs. Nesbit's infidelity, shot her to death, then jumped from the old Gidginbilla Dam into the Castlereagh River. It was a tragedy that aroused Brit's compassion because she held her own father in high regard.

Jimmy set about winning Brit. He wrote her sonnets and bought her trinkets and made promises. He reasoned if he could only win her favor, then her hand, his continuing fortune would be certain as Brit's father was wealthy and her dowry was surely considerable.

Brit was taken aback by the attention lavished upon her by young Jimmy Nesbit. He was kind and understanding and never once tried to push her into compromising her ideals. It wasn't long before Brit became distracted from her school work and her grade point average slipped to a level unacceptable to her father. Wilton warned that her education came first and, if the trend continued, the money would stop.

Brit quit her job, began to concentrate on her studies, and her grades improved. Still, the time she spent with Jimmy took its toll. Her resolve to finish her schooling waned as she thought of a new life with Jimmy. When Jimmy sensed her feelings were getting the better of her, he calculated his move.

Brit was leaving for the final day of class for the semester when she saw Jimmy walking down the sidewalk, smiling as he approached. He looked so handsome in his cardigan sweater and sporting his little-boy grin. Accepting his invitation to accompany him on a weekend outing to Toowoomba seemed infinitely more delightful than going home to hear a lecture on scholastic achievement from her father.

It was the last week of September and the Carnival of Flowers was in full bloom. Entertainment and dancing in the streets abounded, and the atmosphere was conducive to a fling. Jimmy played the gentleman, as always, during the Blue Arrow Drive tour about the city and even more so when he insisted on separate accommodations for their lodging.

After dinner, they danced all night. Champagne left her sparkling, and Jimmy's eyes shined so bright. He was gallant and so lovingly tender, it was easy for Brit to surrender.

The morning after was as enchanting as the night before. Jimmy slid an omni-faceted diamond, housed in virgin platinum, onto the third finger of her left hand. Her course was charted and her direction made narrow.

If her father would but delight in the way she had chosen, the world and all would be as it should. But Brit knew better. Her joy was overshadowed by the prospect of informing Wilton of her intent to delay her education in favor of matrimony. Wilton had been her Gibraltar in her infancy, her foundation in adolescence, and when she came into her own, her beacon on a precipice of uncertainties. Disappointing him was never her intent, but the die was cast and there was no changing that.

Wilton met young Jimmy the day Brittany introduced him as her betrothed. Wilton disapproved of him and believed him to be a bludger. Jimmy had no career, no job, and lived solely off his inheritance. Just how did he propose to provide for Brittany when the money was gone? Jimmy had no answer. He was from the out-back and was undignified, lacked boldness, education and fitting protocol. Wilton did all he could to persuade Brit the man was beneath her but to no avail. At twenty, she was a head-strong young woman.

Wilton did not attend the wedding in the little chapel, just outside of Burren Junction, in the bush of New South Wales. That was Brit's first heartbreak.

Although annoyed that Wilton had shunned him from the beginning, Jimmy held to his resolve that the enormous Hayes fortune would eventually fall into Brit's keeping. For nearly eight years Jimmy waited. He guided Brit into a sense of financial security as his failed ventures sapped his fortune.

Brit's life was marginally content even though it sorely missed the story-book mark she'd once imagined. During her term as Jimmy's wife, she spent time alone because

Jimmy's dealings often took him away. As years went by he was gone more often than not, but Brit had plenty to occupy herself on their two hundred hectare ranch, fifty kilometers from the town of Burren Junction.

When he finally ran out of money, Jimmy told Brit the truth about their economics. In keeping with her character, Brit was true to her vows and stood by him, for better, and for worse. It was disheartening when she learned the ranch would be sold at auction for tax liabilities, but Brit was a strong woman and accepted the state of affairs. Even so, she couldn't hold back the tears when the horse trailer backed up to the barn and the live stock trader loaded up her prized Arabian mare she'd raised from a foal. By the time all her antiques and furnishings were sold, there was little left to move to the dilapidated cottage on the poor side of Burren Junction.

Brit found a job, scrimped and saved, and tried to pay the bills while Jimmy crawled into a bottle. The fall came swiftly, and with a vengeance. Jimmy wouldn't work, but his grandiose plans never ceased. Brit argued that if he'd just spend half the time seeking a job that he spent concocting ideas to make an easy dollar, they'd soon be on their way. Nothing she said moved him, and he became callous and increasingly bitter.

Tension mounted as things went from bad to worse. One night, after a heated exchange, Jimmy was enraged at Brit's refusal to ask her father for money. It was then when Brit understood what her father meant when he'd said he could see Beelzebub in the eyes of that hoon from the never-never. Jimmy attacked her unmercifully.

When Brit became conscious, she was lost and afraid. Her attending physician explained that an anonymous caller had notified the hospital of the beating and an ambulance was dispatched to her home. Brit didn't know who made the call that saved her life. Neither did she know that during her critical period of recovery, her father sat beside her bed and held her hand with a prayer on his lips and vindication in his heart.

It wasn't until the day before her release from the hospital that Brit learned of Jimmy Nesbit's recompense. She was reclining in bed and waiting for the nurse to bring her supper when the news came over the television. The report stated that the Burren Junction constabulary was perplexed over the incident and unable to decipher why Jimmy's big Weatherby 300 magnum exploded and blew off half his face. It was deemed a freak accident during an illegal hunting expedition near the opal mines just north of Lightening Ridge.

Upon her release, Brit had but one place to turn. Battered and ashamed, she showed up at her father's home, having no money even for cab fare. It was a tearful reunion but Wilton was a comfort. Brit's humiliation eventually faded, and her self-respect gradually returned.

For the next several months, Brit stayed in Brisbane with Wilton. It was a time for reflection, a time to heal, and finally, a time to get on with her life. She resumed her maiden name and resolved to put the past behind. But what would she do? With only two years at the University she had no viable skills to support herself in any semblance of style to which she was once accustomed. Wilton offered continued asylum and opportunity to finish her schooling but Brit was nearly thirty years old with a feeling that life was passing her by.

Brit wanted to see the world and find out just what was on the other side, but that took money, and money was a fleeting commodity. Wilton would have willingly underwritten her desire to take a holiday, but all things considered, she couldn't bring herself to ask him. But unbeknownst to Brit, in his intuitive wisdom,

Wilton provided a way for her at the onset of her youthful rebellion. He'd purchased an endowment policy on Jimmy Nesbit's life and designated her beneficiary the very day she married him. When Brit learned of her unexpected fortune, for the first time in a long time, she savored the smell of freedom.

A month later Brit stepped off the plane and onto American soil at Los Angeles, California. The City of Angels with all its pomp and hustle seemed eons away from the estrangement she'd known for the past ten years on the other side of the world.

After securing her papers through Immigration, she took a job waiting tables at a bistro in Long Beach to busy herself. She rented a flat near her employment and settled into her new life there. She bought a late-model station wagon and enrolled in driving class. It was no small accomplishment, learning to drive on the wrong side of the road with the steering wheel on the awkward side of the vehicle, but soon she became proficient and confident enough to leave L.A. and take to the highway.

Determined to see America, Brit drifted down to San Diego where she found her jumping point. She stood facing the Pacific Ocean and pondered the road sign that read, "Hwy 80 End." One of the interesting ditties in her road

atlas advised that Highway Eighty was the longest highway in the continental United States.
Three months and three thousand miles later
she found herself deliberating an identical sign
and surveying the Atlantic.

    After southern California, Tybee Island
was indeed a breath of fresh air. There were no
clouds of smog choking the city, no polluted
waterways, and no inauspicious rumblings from
the San Andreas fault. Everyone was friendly
and willing to help her feel comfortable on the
island; no one was a stranger there.

    Brit was ecstatic when she found a rea-
sonable rent at the Tybee Island Beach Resort
on the north end of the island. One look and it
felt like home. The grounds were immaculate
with oleanders, palmettos, and grass, mani-
cured as for a showplace. The yard was ablaze
with flowering vincas, impatiens, hibiscus, gar-
denia, and tea olive. Exotic ferns softened the
searing heat, and for a moment, took her back
to plush, tropical gardens on Fraser Island, just
east of Platypus Bay. On holiday she'd made
countless treks to the island with her father.
But that was another lifetime, so very long ago.

    The condominium was small; the upkeep
would be negligible. Her unit was on the third
floor of the "A" building facing the ocean. The

view was best observed from the small but adequate back porch. At any given moment, one might have seen a freight ship carrying its cargo to some exotic port. Brit spent many nights beholding the panoramic scene that scrolled before her eyes. She pondered the ships, the sea, the sky and her destiny.

Fortune again smiled on Brit when she was offered a job in the lounge at the DeSoto Beach Motel. The DeSoto was a sprawling old structure once frequented by the likes of Al Capone. The antiquated buildings gave patrons the subtle suggestion they'd stumbled upon the architectural composite of Old Madrid, Saint Augustine and the Alamo. The exterior walls were bone-colored with green and orange trim and the leak-plagued roof was fashioned of terracotta tile. From years of neglect the well-seasoned resort had fallen into a state of disrepair but refurbishing was under way, and there were rumors of plans for a new addition.

The Shipwatch Lounge, known locally as the "Shipwreck," was a popular spot for vacationers, an array of Tybee Islanders, and center stage for the continuing saga, "As Tybee Turns." Working there would keep her in the thick of things, and she'd heard the tips were good during the season. Her hours were eight to five and that suited her just right.

It was good getting up early, having breakfast, and reporting for work that first morning.
Brit sat in the lounge, waited to punch the time
clock, and watched the sun burn a trail across
the eastern sky and rise high over the ocean.
The lounge's plate glass windows needed a good
cleaning. Dried ocean mist had left a white,
filmy residue that detracted from the pictur-
esque view of the Atlantic.

At precisely eight o'clock, Gloria, the head
waitress, bounded through the kitchen door and
into the lounge. She introduced herself, and
smiled as she hurried round the huge horse-
shoe bar, tying her apron as she came. She
was glad to see Brit. The place had been a mad
house since the season began, and it was damn
time they got her some more help.

Gloria was a bundle of energy, always on
the go. She worked two full-time jobs, determined to get her son through medical school,
whatever the cost. When she wasn't working at
the Shipwreck, she was manager of the produce
department at the Kroger store on Wilmington
Island.

Her hair was cut in a shag, spiked on top,
and colored bottle-blonde. It contrasted sharply
with her Cherokee skin and the blue dolphin

tattoo behind her left shoulder.   She wore shorts, moccasins, a DeSoto tank-top, and took quick little steps that propelled her at remarkable speed around the Shipwreck. She was friendly, helpful and kept a good attitude in spite of her aching back and hectic schedule.

Gloria took pleasure introducing Brit to her new workplace and to her duties. She took pleasure in everything she did. Brit liked her from the beginning, and the sentiment was mutual.

Gloria instructed Brit that her first task of the morning would be a daily ritual: Make a Bloody Mary. Gloria handed a bottle of Tobasco across the bar and directed Brit to garnish the drink with a lime wedge and to heat it up. Sam liked it spicy. Brit stood a moment, puzzled, and awaited Gloria's explanation. The drink was for Sam Lewis; he lived in the cabana. She'd find him sitting in his chair where he sat every morning.

After doctoring the drink, Brit stirred it with a swizzle stick, touched the stick to her lips and sampled the mixture. She gave Gloria the high sign, placed the drink on a service tray and headed for the eastern door. On her way she again noticed the dirty picture windows and wondered if, between her charges, she might find time to scour them down.

Brit walked outside and up the wooden ramp that led to the tiki bar and sun deck. Several guests were lounging by the pool, and some small children were arguing with their mothers about going into the water so soon after breakfast. The place would presently be alive with guests but as yet the deck was fairly quiet.

Brit spotted a man sitting alone with steepled hands resting against his chin. His feet were propped on the wooden bench that surrounded the deck and he gazed pensively across the water. He wore dingy white tennis shorts and amber sun glasses. His hair was wind-blown and his tanned back glistened with perspiration from the new sun. If he heard her approaching, he gave no indication.

Brit placed the cocktail beside him. When he looked up she smiled that brilliant smile Sam grew to love so much. When she spoke that Aussie rhythm, he hung on every line. It seemed like ages ago, and it seemed like only yesterday.

4

There wasn't much cargo space in Sam's vintage 1965 Mustang but it was sufficient;

there wasn't much to haul. Sam packed his clothes, a couple of blankets, and a box of bachelor-food into the trunk. He shoved everything to the left, then angled in a styrofoam cooler stuffed with everything else. It took three good slams before the lock engaged and he got it all in. He arranged his diving equipment in the back seat, set his miniature ghetto blaster and Jimmy Buffet tape collection in the front, then went to the motel office to settle up.

He paid his bill and went outside to count his cash. He had enough money, without going into his bank account, to take him to the Keys and keep him situated until he could make the right contacts and find something to do.

Sam settled into the driver's seat, fired the engine, slid a cassette into the slot of the ghetto blaster and pressed the play button. He drove out onto Highway 80, turned right, and wound the gears as he sped down the road, unaware Brit was watching him.

As he drove away he was tormented. Overcoming his fears and deciding to ask Brit to be his wife had been no simple matter for Sam. Years before, someone hurt him badly, and the scars ran deep. There was no pain like a heartache and Sam never wanted to know that feeling again.

Sam thought of the first time he asked Brit to be his wife. It was late Sunday night on December 23 down by the south jetties. They'd decided to go for a walk on the beach so he took her hand and they made their way to the water. A fast-moving cold front had set in, and winter was displaying its true colors, but Brit was toasty in her blue ski suit with the cozy fleece hood.

They walked two miles to the sea wall at the mouth of the Back River, the Savannah River's little sister, that defined Tybee's southern shore line. The tide was low and the jetties stretched two hundred feet before disappearing beneath the churning salinity of the Atlantic. Brit and Sam gazed over the ocean at the merchant ships that were lined up in the shipping channel. The vessels waited for the pilot boats to ferry the river pilots to their helms and facilitate passage to the Port of Savannah. Brit counted seven of them. Together they stood in the silvery moonlight, hand in hand, and Sam gazed at the moon's reflection that twinkled in her eyes.

When the decision was made, and the question asked, the answer gave no surprise. Sam didn't blame Brit. How could he? He knew

her past. She was afraid and that was under-
standable. But Sam never gave up hope, not
until the previous night when she told him she
didn't know if the answer would ever change.
Even then, Sam would have stayed and just
loved the part of her she was willing to give, but
preserving his sanity had to be primary. He
was only a man, and if reduced to babbling lu-
nacy, then where was his worth?

When Sam reached Arnie's Beach Store
he whipped into the parking lot and pulled to
the gas pumps. After filling up he walked inside. He gathered a carton of cigarettes, two
Butterfinger candy bars, a large black coffee,
and placed everything on the counter. He stood
in line at the cash register and absently stared
at the floor.

He thought of the Lazaretto Creek Bridge
he'd cross when leaving the island. He'd only
crossed it four times since he first came to Tybee.
There'd been no reason to. Everything he'd ever
needed or wanted was right there at home.

Sam had crossed under the bridge,
though, many times. He remembered when Brit
sat beside him at the helm of the boat as they
passed under the bridge on their way to open
ocean. They were going to the Snapper Banks
for their first dive trip together.

Brit was everything to Sam. She was in his thoughts every waking hour, and then, she danced in his dreams. She filled the void of a man standing alone against the world. Now, there was an emptiness inside him which made that void seem abundant.

Sam returned to his car, set the grocery bag on the floorboard, and adjusted the mirror. He cranked the engine, shoved the shifter in gear, and let off the clutch. The car barely rolled when a white Mercedes with dark tinted windows came screeching to a halt and nearly rammed the front of his car. Sam slammed the brakes and the coffee went into his lap. Angrily, he jumped from his car and started for the Mercedes.

"What are you, nuts!" he yelled at the offender.

"Yes!" he heard a voice that instantly softened his demeanor.

The Mercedes' door opened and Brit stood from the car. Slowly, she walked Sam's way. Her look was intent and deliberate. Her lips again quivered and her voice trembled when she spoke.

"Yes," she said. "I will marry you," she put her arms around Sam and held him fast.

"Brit, I..."

"Hush," she sobbed. "Just hold me, Sam'o...please hold me."

Sam buried his face into her hair and comforted her. After a time, she looked into his eyes and her tears gave way to gladness. Sam wiped her cheek and brushed her hair from her face.

"Forgive me for what I've put you through," Brit said with a certain purity. "I've been such a fool."

"There's nothing to forgive, my love. And you could never be a fool."

"I've always loved you, Samuel Quincey Lewis. I guess I never knew how very much until I saw you driving out of my life. I was prepared to follow you all the way to Islamorada if I had to," Brit said. "I'm glad you stopped at Arnie's."

"Where did you get the car?" Sam asked in an attempt to lighten the moment.

Brit chuckled a bit. "I couldn't find my purse nor my car keys so I borrowed it from Jerry. It's brand new, he just bought it."

"That's a high-dollar ride. I'll bet he'd have been upset if you didn't return," Sam said, smiling.

"He gave me his credit card and told me to get after it. He said to catch you if I can," she smiled back, holding up the card. "Jerry is a true friend."

"Yeah," Sam agreed.

"I feel so relieved," Brit said. "It's as if a terrible burden has been lifted from my shoulders."

"Yeah," Sam held her close a long while then whispered, "Let's get back to the DeSoto, baby. Let's go home."

Sam couldn't keep his eyes on the road during their drive back. His car flanked the Mercedes while they traveled down the highway laughing all the way. When they reached the big curve, where Highway Eighty met the ocean, Sam crossed the center line and nearly ran into oncoming traffic.

Brit and Sam found two parking spots side by side and exited the vehicles. They stood facing each other then Brit threw her arms around him. They embraced another moment then walked toward the Shipwreck's northern door. Once inside, Gloria, bounded their way. A joyful tear trickled down Gloria's cheek as she hugged Brit's neck and whispered "God bless" into her ear. "God bless you both," she said, releasing Brit.

Then, Gloria stepped back, placed her hand on her hip, and eyed Sam with mocked reproof. She pointed her finger and scolded him.

"If you *ever* make this lady cry again, I'll be wearing your scalp around my belt. And *you*, young lady," she turned to Brit. "If you're ever stubborn enough to let this man slip away again, then I just don't know what to do with you. Now, if you two are finished with your little wrangle, we have work to do." Sam and Brit shrugged and laughed. After giving Sam a quick kiss, Brit followed Gloria around the bar. Just as they disappeared into the kitchen, Sam heard a friendly voice.

"Happy Friday." Jerry Kirbo smiled as he rested his pool stick against the wall then shook Sam's hand.

Jerry was a good man. He was in his late-fifties and young at heart. He was never down, and his attitude was always positive. He never said an unkind word to or about anyone.

Whether it was a "Happy Friday," a "Happy Sunday," or a happy day or night, he always wore his rose-colored sun shades through which he viewed his world. He was well traveled, self-assured, and usually offered a philosophical thought that commanded speculation.

His home was an elaborately furnished forty-one foot Hatteras sport fisherman that he moored at Lazaretto Creek. He was Sam's dive buddy. It was on his boat that Brit and Sam had passed under the bridge time and again.

"Happy Friday to you," Sam grinned.

"You're one lucky man. Here's to you," Jerry tipped his bottle of Miller Lite and finished the last swallow. He dropped the empty bottle into the trash then walked back toward his favorite pool table. Sam followed as Jerry went his way.

Jerry chalked his stick and looked for his best shot. "And she's a lucky girl," he took careful aim at the five ball. He struck the cue ball with his stick and there came a loud smack when the cue ball collided with the five. The five flew into the left-corner pocket and the cue ball lined up on the eight.

"Brittany is crazy about you, Sam," Jerry straightened up from the table and faced Sam. "You should have seen her running around here in a panic when she couldn't find her keys. I'd just come back to the island with that car right after you left."

"Thanks, Jerry. She got there in the nick of time. I was heading for the bridge," said Sam.

"Don't mention it," Jerry chalked his stick again. "Brittany is a good girl, Sam. Treat her right. I've gotten to know her well and she's very special to me.

"Yeah, you're lucky all right. I've seen a lot of men hit on her but she always puts them in their place. And you know what I like about her? She does it with style. Aussie style. Why, if I didn't like you so much, I'd cut you up into little pieces, feed you to the crabs, and marry her myself," Jerry ribbed him.

"You got a way with words, you know that, Jerry?"

Jerry took aim at the eight and slammed the cue ball with his stick. The eight streaked home to the side pocket and Jerry returned his stick to the rack.

"You might have a tiger by the tail there, buddy. I get the feeling she's not one to take any guff off anybody, not anymore anyhow. If you don't treat her right, she just might drag you round and round that skinny old palm tree and spin you into butter," Jerry looked out the Shipwreck's eastern window and motioned toward a sickly palmetto. The tree stood near the water's edge and looked ravaged by a sea beaver.

"Not to worry, my friend. She's in the best of care."

"I know she is," Jerry said with a look of surety. "Just make her proud of you, Sam...always make her proud. If she's proud, then you know you're on the right track. If she's not, then you know you're a shit."

"Thanks for the wise words, Jerry. Thought provoking as always. I hate to run, but I gotta go."

"Catch you later, Sam." Jerry went to his bar stool and Sam went to the motel office.

If ever there was a contented man, it was Sam Lewis. He checked back into the cabana and unloaded his belongings while he planned a celebration. He bounced back over to the Shipwreck, invited Brit to dinner, then headed for the super market. He hadn't cooked a decent meal since he could remember when. That night he would!

5

By the end of Brit's work shift, the unseasonable crowd had largely diminished. Brit's replacement had called in saying she would be late. Brit wasn't bothered by it. She'd been around the Shipwreck long enough to experience many setbacks in time schedules and she'd quickly adjusted to them. The locals referred to those little setbacks as "Tybee Time." When many Tybee Islanders said they would be someplace at a given time, they weren't generally expected until an hour later.

Gloria emerged from the kitchen carrying a large tub of ice that she agilely dumped into a bin in the central area of the bar. As she lowered the tub she noticed Brit standing at the waitress station slicing limes and placing the slices into a preparation tray that contained cherries, celery sticks, olives, pearl onions, and lemon wedges. Gloria saw there was much on Brit's mind.

"I can do that," Gloria said, approaching the waitress station.

"I don't mind."

"That's one of th' things I like about you, Brittany. You take care of business."

"As it should be," Brit shrugged without looking up.

Gloria watched her a moment, then said, "Big day for you, huh?"

Brit stopped slicing the limes, looked off at the ocean and replied, "Bigger than you know."

"Oh, I think I know. You've just made th' biggest decision of your life. And now that you've taken that great big step, maybe you're wondering if th' next step is on th' edge of something you can't see."

"It shows?"

"Uh huh. And I'll tell you something else.

Only th' candy asses of this world are th' ones who have to know that th' next step is safe."

"I can't help but be nervous, Gloria. It's been a long time for me," Brit said behind a smile as she relaxed a bit.

"Let me tell ya something," Gloria returned the smile, pleased to see Brit's tension ease. "There ain't no guarantees in life. No free lunch," she removed her glasses and cleaned them with a bar napkin. "You and Sam Lewis are like family to me. Maybe I'm steppin' outa' line but what th' hell," she said, replacing her glasses on her face. "You ain't th' only one who took a big step. But th' thing is...Sam took it a while back."

"I...I don't follow you," Brit said honestly.

"Look Brittany...sure, you had one helluva bad experience with that Nesbit asshole. And it took a lot of guts for you to overcome it. We've all had bad experiences from bad choices at one time or another. Sam's been there too."

"He told me about his wife," said Brit.

"Uh, huh. How th' marriage didn't work out? How he put so much time in his business that he neglected her? How he was out of town for so long so many times?"

"Yes, Sam told me all about it."

"Uh, huh, that's Sam...a gentleman all the way."

"Gloria, I think you've lost me once again."

"What I'm saying is, Sam didn't tell you how his little wife felt *so* neglected with him being out of town making money to pay for th' *big house with th' swimming pool*, to buy her *expensive jewelry*, to pay for th' *boat* she wanted, to buy her th' *fine clothes* she had to have, that she turned to Sam's attorney, who was supposedly Sam's friend, to comfort her during all this *neglect*."

Brit eyed her a moment then asked, "Are you saying...?"

"Uh, huh," Gloria interrupted. "Little Miss Priss was busy sharing th' *satin sheets* that Sam was out working so hard to pay for. All the while his wife and his good buddy were leading him down th' primrose path. When they were done with him, he didn't have a pot to piss in or a window to throw it out."

"I...I had no idea," Brit said absently.

"Like I said. Sam's a gentleman. And a *gentle man*," she smiled at Brit and continued. "Count your blessings. It took a lot of guts for him to take that step regarding you. Hell, he could have felt that because of his bad experience he had better not get seriously involved with another woman. Then, my Aussie friend...you would have no doubt missed th' best thing that ever came into your life."

"Well...why didn't you marry him?" Brit asked, attempting to brighten the conversation.

"He never asked," Gloria replied. "If he had, I'd be throwing rocks at you every time you came around," she added with a wink.

Brit's eyes moistened with relief. She leaned across the bar and gave Gloria an awkward hug.

"You don't know what you've just done," Brit said, wiping her eyes and gaining back her composure.

"Maybe not. But I'd sorta like to think that maybe I pointed out that th' Big Guy in th' sky looked down on you two and said, Yeah, that'll work."

"I don't know how to thank you."

"You can thank me by loving Sam Lewis just as hard as you can. He deserves you...and you him," Gloria said, placing her hand on Brit's.

"The good thing about that is, if it's a contest...we both win," Brit smiled with a different sparkle in her eye.

"Good. Now, don't worry about staying here. I can handle it. You go and make yourself pretty for your man," Gloria said, handing Brit her purse from behind the bar.

"Thank you again, Gloria."

"If th' first kid's a girl...what are you gonna name her?" Gloria asked with a sly look.

"Well, if it's okay with Sam'o...I'd like to name her after my mom."

"Oh. I can understand that. But you know...I was sorta hopin'...Ah, forget it."

Brit placed her arms around Gloria's neck, then gave her the warmest of smiles.

"My mom's name was Gloria."

6

Sam sharpened his knife on his stone, honed it with his steel, and sliced up the beginnings of what would be an enchanting evening. There'd be wine and candles and soft music, but best of all there'd be Brit, wonderful Brit. Was it real or was it all only a dream? He'd seen a lot of dreams decay into reality.

Sam had a lot to think about now that there was someone to care for other than himself. Obtaining gainful employment was the first order of business on his agenda. That shouldn't be much of a problem, judging from the number of building permits issued on Tybee, according to the newspaper. The next day he'd take a ride around the island and scout it out.

The last job he'd worked was in Atlanta and it lasted a little over three years. He'd been awarded the plumbing contract on a new regional medical center that made him a bundle. After overseeing an industrial project of that magnitude, anything he might find on Tybee would be a piece of cake.

Sam had enough money stashed away and his investments were such that he could spend the next couple of years in semi-retirement if he wanted. That put him in a good position to pick and choose any jobs he might care to bid on. He could quote the work at a premium price, and if he didn't get it, he really didn't care. If he did receive a contract, it would be worth his while.

Now, things were going to be different. Sam wanted to make a home for Brit, and one day, maybe even for little Sammy. He wanted to give Brit the opportunity to decide whether she wanted to work or not. Maybe she might want to complete her degree or perhaps start some new career. He wanted her to enjoy life and feel secure in the knowledge that her husband was a good provider. She deserved that. That's the way it should be, he thought, and provide for her he would.

7

At five minutes of eight, dinner was on the table, illuminated with candle light and accented by a vase holding three red roses. The meal was Sam's equivalent of a New England clam-bake, but with a low-country twist:

Split Maine lobster stuffed with deviled crab, lobster stew, cherry stone clams with melted butter, new potatoes, asparagus with Hollandaise sauce, and a chilled bottle of Vouvray.

Precisely at eight o'clock, Brit knocked on the door. She was stunning, her hair piled high upon her head. The most beautiful ruby lips and glistening emerald eyes were smiling at him as she walked into the room. Her short black dress was cut to be modestly revealing. It was just tight enough to accent her lovely form but not so tight as to invite provocation.

"It smells wonderful," Brit said as she placed her tote bag on the credenza.

"It surely does," Sam agreed, her perfume filling his nostrils.

"What are we having?" she asked.

Sam turned out the overhead light, took her hand, and led her to the table.

"Oh, Sam'o, it's all so lovely," she said and

kissed his cheek.

He helped her with her chair, poured the wine, then offered a toast.

"To you Brit. To us, and to new beginnings."

She clinked her wine glass against his, then they dined on the meal Sam worked so hard to prepare just right. The lobster was succulent, the crab, seasoned to perfection, and the asparagus was creamy rich.

After they did the dishes and put everything away, they laughed, and danced and passed away the night. Life relinquished its demands and the space in time was theirs alone.

At a quarter of twelve, the Johnny Mathis tape had long-since ended and the candles were beginning to flicker. Brit and Sam continued holding one another as they slowly danced around the room. To them, the world was like the tape: still and quiet. Neither Sam nor Brit knew how long it had been since they had last spoken. Nor did they realize how long they'd been dancing to the rhapsody that came from their souls.

Some time later, they stopped dancing, then Brit separated slightly from Sam. When he looked into her searching eyes, he felt them pierce him. After what seemed an eternity, Brit slowly moved backward and locked the door. Those wonderful eyes were then ablaze, never leaving his. She hesitated a moment, then moved toward Sam. She drew him to her and kissed him, kindling his hunger, igniting the flame. His longing gave way to urgency; excitement within them churned. He savored her essence, she breathed his breath.

Brit took Sam's hand and led him to the bedroom. She turned and faced him as she took the pins from her hair and shook her head, freeing her golden locks, that flowed down and round her shoulders. With a single fluid movement, she undid her satin dress and it slipped down her body and onto the floor. What Samuel Quincey Lewis beheld at that moment was the closest thing to rapture he had ever known.

At once, they were in fiery embrace. Brit quivered at the touch of his hand, so gentle, yet so intense. She uttered his name as she kissed him, hot breath quickening, fervor churning, burning like the phoenix rising from the ashes of her forgotten desire.

The adrenaline pumped through every fiber that was Sam Lewis. He could feel the inferno that raged inside her, and the desire to be engulfed in that flame consumed him.

With unparalleled feeling she licked her lips as he drew ever closer. Their emotions were as molten lead as their bodies melded into one. It was nearly dawn when they collapsed exhausted onto the mattress. With complete abandon, they held one another until the tide they'd shared reached its ebb. Then they slept. Brit knew it was right. If the old adage, "Home is where the heart is," was indeed true, then she was surely home.

8

Just before ten o'clock Saturday morning, Sam rolled over to hold Brit but she was gone. He sat bolt upright and called her name. For a moment he feared the night before was only a dream but then he saw the note on the night stand.

"Good morning, luv. Hope I didn't disturb you when I left," it read. "I tried to be quiet as a mouse. See you soon. Love, me."

Sam smiled as he returned the note to the table. He fell back onto the bed and reached for her pillow. Her fragrance graced the pillow case and Sam lingered there a while relishing her scent. Momentarily, he rose from the bed and went to the bathroom. Her dress, stockings, and tote bag hung neatly from the hook on the back of the door, and her tooth brush rested next to his in the plastic cup on the lavatory. Sam whistled a happy tune as he stepped into the shower.

After his bath, Sam dressed and made a pot of coffee. Three doughnuts and five cups of java later, he was ready to face the day. The gulls were screeching like always, but somehow that morning, they sounded like they were singing.

"Mornin' birds," Sam said after stepping outside with the remainder of his stale breakfast. He crumbled the doughnuts one by one and threw them to the gulls, then followed his usual path. He walked the steps, went to his chair, propped up his feet and waited for his Bloody Mary.

After a moment he heard someone approaching. The footsteps were familiar but they weren't Brit's. Every other step was accompanied by the unmistakable clank of a metal crutch. When Sam heard the raspy voice shouting his name, he readied himself for the barrage of obscenities and stale ribbings he knew would follow.

"Sam Lewis, you son of a bitch, I've been

looking for you."

Sam turned his head to find Clyde Gray, walking toward him with an extended hand.

"Clyde, you old sea dog. How the hell are you?" Sam stood for the handshake.

"Busy. How about yourself?" Clyde shifted his crutch to a more comfortable position.

"You see it. Just another day in paradise. What can I say?" Sam smiled.

"Still ain't workin', huh? Must be nice."

"Well, I did finally finish those plans for my off-shore dive platform, gambling casino, and whorehouse I've been dreamin' about. I could use somebody to bankroll me. What do you say Clyde?" Sam said with a grin. "Want a piece of the action?"

"That's exactly what you need, a whorehouse. It'd be nice to see you with some *classy* ladies for a change," Clyde slapped him on the back and it stung like it always did when Clyde was up to something he thought clever.

Clyde was a structural engineer as well as a builder. He'd been the general contractor on Sam's hospital job in Atlanta and was a close friend. He was forty-five years old with a medium build. His sandy hair was slightly balding, and he wore a well-trimmed mustache. His crutch was the result of a drunken car crash twenty years before and a constant reminder of youthful stupidity in the fast lane. Clyde liked nothing better than having a little laugh, usually at Sam's expense.

Just then, Clyde reacted to Brit as she gracefully negotiated through the crowd expertly balancing her drink-laden tray.

"Now look at that one, buddy. She'd make a preacher kick out a stained glass window. That's enough to turn any man's head."

"She's okay," Sam said, leading him on.

"Okay! You been kicked in the head or something?"

"Sure, she looks good but she just isn't my type," Sam said, doing well to keep a straight face.

"Damn right she ain't your type. You couldn't get to first base with a looker like that."

"I wouldn't be so sure of myself if I were you, Clyde."

Clyde looked at Sam with a mischievous grin, then reached into his pocket and removed a wad of money. He peeled off a hundred dollar bill, dropped it to the table, and secured it with an empty beer bottle left there by someone the night before.

"I got a hundred bucks that says she'll

sluff you off like water rolls off a duck's back."

"Come on. I don't wanna take your money," Sam said, reeling him in.

"What's the matter? You lettin' your alligator mouth overload your puppy-dog ass?"

"All right, if you insist. But don't say I didn't warn you."

Brit finished serving the couple at the end of the deck, then headed in Clyde's and Sam's direction. Before she had the chance to speak, Sam addressed her.

"Pardon me, Miss. May I have a moment of your time?" Sam said, with a wink.

"Certainly, sir," Brit replied, quick with her wits.

"You are, without a doubt, the most marvelous creature I have ever seen on this green earth," said Sam.

"Why, thank you, mate. You are too kind," Brit replied and mimed a slight curtsey.

"And your eyes," Sam continued, "like limpid pools, are windows to your inner beauty," Clyde looked on, his mouth wide open.

"And your lips are surely soft, red and sweet, as a bowl of cherries," Brit swooned, superbly playing the role.

"I'm not a well man. I don't know how long I have, but now I can die fulfilled. After seeing you I am convinced. There truly *is* a God.

"If I may be so brazen, could I beg from you the profound honor of a simple kiss...a remembrance of this moment?"

Brit casually set Sam's Bloody Mary on the table beside the hundred dollar bill.

"Here mate, hold this," Brit shoved the empty tray into Clyde's stomach. She threw both arms around Sam, wrapped one leg around his, buried her mouth on Sam's, and gave him a long, exaggerated kiss, then she turned to Clyde.

"Beg your pardon, mate, may I get you something?" she asked, casually reclaiming her tray.

"Yeah," said Clyde. "A stiff belt of Georgia moonshine would go down real good right now."

Pleased with the ultimate payback for years of Clyde's ribbing, Sam could no longer keep a straight face. He broke into laughter as he bent down and picked up the hundred dollars. He put his arm around Brit's waist and through his chortle, made his confession.

"Baby, I'd like you to meet my old friend, Clyde Gray. Clyde, this is Brittany Hayes, my fiancée."

"The pleasure's all mine, Brittany," Clyde offered his hand looking embarrassed and bewildered.

"G'day Clyde. Lovely to meet you." Brit

gave Sam a quick kiss, then excused herself and hurried back toward the Shipwreck. It was another busy day. Sam and Clyde watched her every move as she walked away.

"Well I'll swear and be damned," Clyde declared, now starting to laugh a little himself. "I didn't think you had it in you, Sam. You can just call that c-note a wedding gift. This joke's on me."

"Thank you, I will."

"Congratulations buddy. If I hadn't seen it with my own eyes, I'd never have believed it. Damn, she's pretty."

"And you know what else, Clyde," Sam smiled as he watched Brit disappear into the Shipwreck. "She's just as sweet as she is pretty. There ain't a mean bone in her body."

Clyde shifted his crutch again and smiled back at Sam. His coarse demeanor softened as he spoke. "I'm happy for you. I always knew there was someone out there for you somewhere."

"Yeah," Sam said thoughtfully. "But you know what's funny? She didn't come along until I decided to quit looking."

"That's the way it works my friend," Clyde nodded. "That's the way it works.

"Now, there's something I want to talk to you about," said Clyde.

"What's on your mind?"

"I've got an ass-load of work coming up on Tybee. How'd you like to lay some pipe for me?"

"Sounds interesting, whatcha got going?"

"Come on. Grab your drink, let's take a little ride and I'll show you."

That little ride proved interesting indeed. Clyde told Sam he'd disbanded Gray Construction's corporate offices and sold his industrial contracts. He was planning to move from Augusta to the house he'd recently bought on Tybee Island. The house sat just across the street from the DeSoto beside the water tower.

Clyde was tired of the stress that came with the responsibility of overseeing heavy construction. He'd built his share of schools, hotels, prisons, and multi-story structures that crept toward the sky.

The sight of concrete and steel monoliths, stacked one upon the other, was not nearly so soothing as the view from his deck on Tybee. He had invested his money wisely. He could retire but construction was in his blood. There were more major industrial jobs Clyde would do before taking down his shingle altogether, but for then, his intention was to build an exclusive residential community on the island.

They rode west down Highway 80, past

Arnie's Beach Store, and turned right on the road that went right by Brit's condo. A mile and a half farther on was an eleven-acre tract of partially cleared land bordering the Savannah River. The job-site was teeming with bulldozers, pans, and motor-graders.

Clyde pulled his blue Chevy Silverado pick-up to the side of the road, reached behind the seat for a huge set of blue prints, then he and Sam exited the vehicle. Clyde spread open the plans across the hood of his truck and smiled proudly.

The prints called for a seven-story high-rise condominium complex complete with a health club, hair salon, and members-only restaurant. In addition there would be a swimming pool, club house, tennis court, and a guard shack. No detail had been omitted and no expense was to be spared in the ambitious project. Sam was impressed.

"This job will be a walk in the park," Clyde said as he folded up the drawings. The county building inspectors around here don't ride you like they do in Atlanta or Augusta or Macon. What do you say, Sam? You wanna ram-rod the plumbing on this little job?"

"I don't come cheap you know."

"You never did. We'll work the same deal as always. I'll provide you with a payroll allowance for you to hire your labor, and I'll give you six figures for the next twelve months of your time."

"All right, Clyde It'll be good to be back in the saddle again." Sam smiled and extended his hand. "You've got yourself a deal."

"Good. I'll draw up the contract."

"When will you be ready for me?" asked Sam, anxious to get started.

"It's going to be two weeks before I get the main building laid out and the footings poured so you can run the underground," Clyde told him. "You'd better enjoy the rest of your little vacation cause it's balls to the walls after that."

Clyde dropped Sam off at the DeSoto, then raced down the highway. As he walked toward the Shipwreck, Sam's head was spinning from a twenty-four-hour whirlwind. He picked up his pace and jogged toward the lounge, anxious to tell Brit.

Sam trotted through the northern entrance and spotted Brit sitting at a booth by the windows eating her lunch. It was barely noon, and the place was crowded with regulars and tourists alike. Brit was the only waitress scheduled to work that morning. The management wasn't expecting an April crowd in January so they were caught short-handed. Gloria had just arrived for back-up so Brit took a few minutes to have a sandwich.

"G'day, Sam'o," she greeted him, covering her mouth with her napkin. "Where have you been?"

"I got a job."

"Good on you, luv! Sit down and tell me about it."

Brit was thrilled and surprised when she learned of Sam's employment. She knew the kind of money Sam could command but it really didn't hit home with her until that morning. And yes, she would quit her job one day to pursue other interests and perhaps start a family.

Brit thought she must be the luckiest shiela on Tybee. Sam's new job would make it much more comfortable when time to tell her father about Sam. It made her queasy just thinking about telling him. But it had to be done and the sooner the better.

"Why don't you come to my place tonight about nine o'clock," said Brit. "We'll have dinner, then we'll ring up daddy and tell him the news."

"How do you think he'll take it?"

Brit shuddered a bit. "I don't want to think too much about it just yet. There'll be time enough for that tonight."

Brit finished her sandwich, rose from the table, kissed her man, then went back to her work.

Sam found his favorite spot at the bar and ordered an O.F.C. and Coke. He was sitting there admiring Brit and watching her wait tables when he felt a hand on his shoulder, then heard, "Happy Saturday." Sam looked behind him and into rose-colored glasses.

"Happy Saturday, Jerry."

"I've never seen you shine so bright," Jerry smiled approvingly.

"I've got a date with an angel."

"Hmmm," Jerry scratched his chin and looked toward Brit. "I saw that same gleam in Brittany's eye earlier when she brought me my Miller Lite. Could it be your hearts are singing the same melody?"

"Ain't she something?" Sam asked, watching her every move.

"She's something all right. And she's really proud of you too. That's good. She told me about your new job."

"Yeah. Things just keep getting better and better for us. Say, by the way, I'm going to be needing some help when the time comes. You don't know anybody who wants to work, do you?"

"Around here? You've got to be kidding."

"Yeah," Sam chuckled. "I know. Everybody is on Tybee Time."

"Well, you could set up a drug and alcohol table on your job-site. Then the dregs that hang out at some of the bars on the island would jump at the chance," Jerry laughed.

"Very funny, Jerry. But you're right. It seems Tybee's labor pool has no bottom."

"What are you looking for?"

"A good helper, that's all. Somebody who'll show up on time for work everyday clean and sober. I know a damn good laborer I'm going to call, and Clyde Gray is bringing down a Johnny-on-the-spot plumber who worked for me in Atlanta."

"How much experience does this helper need?"

"Doesn't matter, really. I just need somebody with a little common sense who wants to work and is willing to learn."

How much are you paying for a green helper with a good head on his shoulders?"

"Seven bucks an hour for thirty days. After that, he'll either get a dollar raise or his walking papers."

"I'll take it."

"Excuse me?"

"I said I'll take the job. Believe it or not, I get bored fishing, diving, drinking beer and watching girls all the time. Besides you've got enough to worry about, running the job and planning your wedding and all. You don't need to be worrying about finding somebody you can count on."

"Jerry. I said seven...eight dollars an hour tops. I wouldn't feel right paying you that."

"If that's what a green helper makes, that's what I want to be paid."

"I appreciate the offer, but why would you want to work for peanuts when you're comfortably retired?"

"If it makes you feel any better, call it a wedding gift."

"Damn, Jerry. I don't know what to say."

"You're hired would be apropos," Jerry smiled.

Sam thought for a moment then said, "okay, you're hired."

"Give me a couple of days notice and I'll be there when you need me. See ya," Jerry said as he turned and walked out the eastern door to the deck.

9

The door to unit three-twenty-seven was standing open when Sam walked inside. The radio was playing soft and low and the smell of Italian seasoning was heavy in the air. He went into the kitchen and found Brit stirring a pot of spaghetti sauce. A bowl of green salad was sitting on the counter next to a freshly baked loaf of bread. The stainless steel top on a boiling pot of water, soon to be filled with vermicelli, rattled on the stove. On the table was a festive service for two.

"Look at you, Brit, where did you find the time..."

Startled, she spun around and faced him. "Oh Sam'o!" she exclaimed, grabbing her heart. "You nearly frightened me to death. I didn't hear you come in," she wrapped her arms around him.

"I'm sorry, baby, I'll knock next time. Look at everything here, you're amazing. How can you make love all night, work all day, and lay out a spread like this?"

"Nothing to it. After work I motored to town and did a bit of shopping. When I returned, I took a short nap, then went to Tybee Market and picked up a few things. After that, I threw

dinner together, then hopped into the bath.
Now, here we are. I hope you're hungry," she
said, removing the top from the pot and pouring in the vermicelli. "Now go and occupy yourself while I finish up."

Sam wandered around the condo while he
waited for supper. Brit's unit was like all the
other units at the complex. It was furnished
with the same furniture that had been put there
when the place was constructed two years previous. Her front door was like every other front
door, and painted a pale green.

Immediately to the right of the entry way
was the bedroom. Just inside the bedroom and
directly left was the bath. Across the hall and
behind a curtain were two bunk beds. At the
end of the hall and to the right was the petite
galley kitchen with a small stove, a stainless
steel sink, a dishwasher, and a refrigerator.

Just past the kitchen was the living area
and beyond that, through the glass sliding door,
was the back porch where Brit and Sam loved
to sit and pass the time. The entire condominium was finished in cheap, pine paneling.
The structure of the two buildings that were the
Tybee Island Beach Resort was modular. The
shell of each unit was constructed in a factory
and shipped in on a flat bed truck. The units

were piled one atop the other by a crane and stacked three high. They were then framed about with wooden siding and stained light-gray. A mansard roof with blue asphalt shingles capped the whole thing off. Brit's home was a fourteen-by-sixty manufactured house on the low end of the market, but with a view of all eternity.

"Now, come have a seat and let me serve you," Brit called to him after a fashion. "This thin spaghetti only takes a few minutes to cook."

Sam washed his hands, sat at the table and watched her move around the kitchen while she filled their plates and took care to make dinner as attractive as she hoped it would be delicious. She set the bread and garnished platters down in front of him, filled the salad bowls, and poured them each a glass of burgundy.

"There now, dig in," she said, adjusting her chair to suit her.

Dinner was superb. The vermicelli was done just right, the sauce correctly seasoned, and the salad, crisp and delicious. Sam took a slice of bread and sopped up the remaining sauce from his plate, carefully absorbing the last little bite.

"Are you sure you've had enough?" Brit asked, wiping her mouth with the cloth napkin.

"Brit, you are an angel. I keep pinching myself, hoping I won't wake up."

"You're not asleep, Sam'o."

She touched his hand a moment, then leaned over and lightly kissed him. After a short time, she rose from the table and began clearing away the dishes. Sam stood to help her but she wouldn't have it.

After cleaning up, Brit wanted to go for a stroll. She and Sam walked to the northern breezeway and stopped a while at the balcony before going down to the water. From the west, the swimming pool's glimmering blue hue, projected by artificial light, was in sharp contrast to the blackness of the night sky. From the pool deck, a long, wooden walkway bridging white sand and amber marsh grass led to a pier that ended on a quiet beach alongside the Savannah River channel.

They endured the northeast wind, bundled up in their winter wear, clinging together. Walking across the weathered planks at low tide, and listening to the popping sounds of marsh dwelling little sand creatures, made them wonder what was really round about them on that bridge to the water. As they made their way to the end of the board-walk, and to the platform overlooking the rushing current, they were entranced by the beauty of it all.

Just across the river lay the state of South Carolina and the Isle of Daufuskie. East of Daufuskie, the lights of Hilton Head glistened in the night and shone across the water like jewels upon the sea. In the distance, the droning of a fishing boat's diesel engines became louder as the vessel churned down the channel and out to the Atlantic. Down by the water's edge a lone couple huddled close against the frigid air as they strolled along the sand. Their senses were filled with fresh salty balm, and their eyes watered as they braved the cold wind confronting them on their easterly travail.

Brit and Sam watched in silence from the pier as the two disappeared down the beach and around the bend. They wondered about the couple. Who were they, and what brought them to this place? Were they lovers? Were they in love? Had they come to this healing ground to mend a dilemma that had invaded their lives? Was there some enigma tormenting them that brought them to Tybee that they might understand, that they could make sense of, so they may reconcile the reasoning behind the circumstance that brought them there?

"You know, Brit, there's something magical about this island." Sam nudged her neck with his nose. "We both came to Tybee to find ourselves and then we found each other. I don't believe it was coincidence, I believe it was fate."

"I know you're right," Brit smiled. "The Almighty surely had His hand in it."

She stood facing him, devoted, wrapped in his arms, drawing from his warmth. Her eyes sparkled as she gazed upon him, wanting him, trusting him, feeling his strength surround her. They kissed. Her lips were soothing as the red wine they had shared, soft as a baby's sigh.

Again, it seemed, the world was theirs alone. There they lingered a long while, each unaware that the other was silently thanking their Creator, for the precious gift of one another. And for the greatest of all things, the gift of love. The temperature was dropping and the wind, like cold blue steel, cut them through.

"It's time," Brit said. "It's afternoon down under."

10

Brit was anxious as she paced before Sam with her "walk-about-telly" cradled on her shoulder. Intermittently, she smiled as she glanced Sam's way. Her eyes lit up when her father answered the phone.

"Daddy," she said, radiating love and ado-ration. "Yes it's me...it's lovely to hear your voice too. How's the weather in Oz?"

Her eyes focused distantly on nothingness as she listened to her father's reply. Sam watched her intently for the few long minutes they talked. He noted every breath, every subtle movement that might tell Wilton's acceptance or rejection of him.

"That's right, daddy...I didn't call just to talk about the weather," she took a deep breath. "I called to tell you I'm getting married."

There was a long pause. Brit's eyes searched for Sam's and found them.

"His name is Sam Lewis."

Sam could only surmise the other side of the conversation. He listened as Brit told her fa-ther how she met Sam and what he did for a liv-ing. She explained how her deep-rooted fears of the past had nearly cost her the man she loved with all her heart.

There were times during their conversation when Sam thought he might walk out on the bal-cony and give Brit a little privacy. But Brit's eyes continuously darting to his, seemingly in need of support, negated that thought. Sam wasn't one to be easily rattled, but as he watched the woman he loved going through the ordeal, he tasted pasta sauce trying to creep back up his throat. He nearly failed his attempt to retain his supper as their conversation became more poignant.

"I'm not asking your permission, daddy. I merely want your blessing," she stated defensively.

Sam stiffened, wondering if he would inadvertently be the instrument to put asunder the relationship between Brit and her father. But worse, what if her love wasn't strong enough to overcome her father's objections? Then, he thought pragmatically, did he or anyone have the right to come between Brit and her father?

Perplexity reined the remainder of the conversation. Sam had lost the ability to follow every word, perhaps even feared doing so. Then, more suddenly than he went into it, Sam was shocked out of his mild state of limbo.

"I'll see you then," Brit said, and hung up the phone.

"He's coming?" Sam asked apprehensively.

"He's coming to America anyway...on business," Brit said, wondering just what sort of business her father had in mind.

"When is he coming?" Sam asked.

"He'll be here March the first. He's chartering a business jet to take him from Brisbane to Savannah. He loathes commercial air-liners."

"That's got to be an expensive way to travel."

"Oh, you don't know daddy. Whatever he does, he does it in a big way."

"What did he say when you told him we were getting married," Sam asked, unsure he really wanted to know. Sam rapidly rose to his feet as Brit walked toward him with outstretched arms.

"Sam'o, I don't know what he's thinking," she said, burying her head into Sam's chest.

"He must have given you some sort of idea."

"That's what puzzles me. Daddy isn't given to be blasé or ambivalent...yet his every question or answer seemed so matter-of-fact."

"Well, baby, maybe we should just wait..."

"Don't you say it, Sam Lewis!" Brit recoiled with fire in her eyes.

"Okay, I won't." Sam forced a weak smile.

"Or even think it." the fire began to cool as she went back to his arms.

"Or think it ever again," Sam added for assurance. "Your love for your father is very important to me, Brit. I don't want to do anything to come between you two."

"You couldn't." she said softly. "God Almighty didn't give me the choice of who my father would be, but he did give me you to be my husband."

"Tell you what," Sam said, trying to be a comfort. "I'll pour us both a glass of wine, you put on Johnny Mathis, and we can snuggle up on the couch and forget about it for a while."

"Thank you, Sam'o," she looked into his eyes. "You always know how to make everything all right."

11

The following afternoon, at two o'clock, Sam walked out of Brit's condominium, down the breeze way, down the stairs and past the pool to the pier. Upon reaching the sandy shore, he turned due east and walked all the way to where the river poured into the ocean. A winter stroll down the beach with no distraction from the summer crowd was most beneficial to one's sense of awareness and solitude.

Down the way he was alone except for an occasional jogger crossing his path. A flock of skimmers, with their lower beaks cutting through the water like turning plows, swiftly passed him, rippling the surface as they strained the ocean for their dinner.

Sam quickened his pace as the birds flew by. Dinner was on his mind also, and just around the bend, and a couple of hundred yards to the south, the DeSoto Beach Motel Sunday afternoon oyster roast was in full swing.

As he walked from the beach and up the wooden ramp to the tiki bar, he saw his enter-tainer friend, Randy Smith, better known as Hat Man Doo, through the Shipwreck window. When he drew closer to the door he sensed the festivity of the standing-room-only crowd. As the door closed behind Sam, Hat Man acknowl-edged him. The bustling crowd, preoccupied with their oysters and their poison, hardly no-ticed when Hat Man crooned a bastardized ver-sion of a popular tune, *"Sam don't know...Sam don't know. Sam don't know where he gonna go, when the hurricane blow."*

Brit heard Hat Man's song and came around the bar to greet Sam, then hurried back to resume her duties. Sam looked around at all the familiar faces and felt at home among the myriad of Tybee Islanders who shared his love for the Shipwreck, for oysters, and for strong drink. When Hat Man finished his song he walked toward Sam, grinning all the while.

"You lucky son of a bitch. I've heard all about it but I won't believe it until I hear it from the horse's mouth. Tell me it ain't so, Sam, tell me it ain't so."

Sam patted him on the shoulder, mocking consolation. "March thirty-first is the big day. Aren't you happy for us?" Sam asked.

"Yeah, I'm happy for you. I just wish I could trade places with you, that's all," Hat Man shook his head and grinned.

"Well, since you can't be the groom, will you settle for best man?"

"Sure, Sam, but only if I don't have to take off my hat. You know I only take it off for two reasons and being your best man ain't one of em."

Randy was a talented musician with the electronic equipment and wherewithal to captivate a crowd and keep them dancing for the four hours or so that he played. He was an entertainer's entertainer and one half of the popular duo, The Two Man Hat Band. He and Charlie Sherrill, a savant with a saxophone, generally played solo. Both were excellent musicians in their own right, but when they teamed up, there was more than just magic.

Hat Man shook his head and walked back to the microphone. As the music started, he spoke to the crowd.

"This one's for the lovely *Britt-naaay*. Soon to be Mrs. Sam Lewis." The song was Brit's favorite, Van Morrison's *Into the Mystic*.

Sam winked at Brit then went over to the

bar. Sitting on his stool at the northeast corner of the Shipwreck was Tom Marshall. Separating Tom and his wife was a hill of oyster shells reflecting an afternoon without worry or care.

Tom was sixty-two years old, going on eighty. And according to his own admission, he was accident prone. His neck was stiff. He told Sam he broke it one night when he fell out of bed. Unfortunately, Tom had suffered a rash of accidents over the past couple of years. In addition to breaking his neck, he fractured his skull one day when he tripped over a foot stool.

He'd broken three fingers when he slammed them in a kitchen drawer, and he nearly died one evening when he inadvertently stabbed himself in the stomach with a butcher knife. Tom always had some sort of injury. He'd have a bandage on his face, a lump on his head, or his arm would be in a sling.

Tom was tall, slender and shaky. But in spite of all his misfortune, he was a jovial old man, always smiling, ready for a joke, though at times oblivious to the world around him. He was nearly deaf and wore a hearing aid in each ear. He always had two days growth of gray whiskers, poking out in all directions from his thin, aging face. His haggard ball cap tilted to one side and his big smile always made one feel comfortable around him.

"Well, well, well, if it ain't Sam Lewis," Tom reared back on his bar stool, smiled widely, and pointed his long, skinny index finger at Sam. "I heard you been a busy boy. First I heard you left for Florida. Then I heard you came back. Now I hear you're marryin' Brittany."

"As Tybee turns," Sam returned the smile. "What are you up to today? And what happened to your eye?" Sam grimaced at the shiner that encompassed Tom's eye socket.

"Well, I'll tell ya my boy. I forgot to duck. And my lovely bride and me are out celebratin' our anniversary. We been together two years today.

"Congratulations," Sam glanced toward Tom's wife, Jan, who was drunk. She twiddled her fingers in a waving gesture and flashed a patronizing simper.

"And ya know what else we're celebratin'?" Tom said proudly. "We're remodelin' our house and yesterday Jan introduced me to feller by the name of Clovis Lark. And he's gonna do the job for a price that's plum fair and reasonable."

"I've never heard of him," said Sam. "What do you know about him?"

"I don't know nothin' about him," said Tom with his steadfast grin. "But my bride says he's okay, and if she says he's okay, then he's okay by me. She says we're givin' the job to Clovis so that's what we're doin', givin' the job to Clovis. Am I right or wrong, Jan?" Tom glanced at his wife for a nod of approval, which he received. Jan took a long draw from her straight vodka and washed down her sixty-third oyster.

"Here, suck down one of these Texas singles." Tom's oyster knife slid through the white flesh that fastened the tender oyster to its mother-of-pearl shell. Sam opened his mouth and accepted the gesture. Cooked just the way Sam liked it, still supple and full of its natural juices, the oyster slid down his throat releasing a bountiful flavor along the way.

Tilting his head forward, Tom looked over the brass frames housing his bi-focals, and said, "Sam, Clovis Lark is a god-send. He's come up with a plan to save me an arm and a leg on my buildin' costs. He's providin' the labor, and I'm overseein' the project. Am I right or wrong, Jan?"

He glanced at his wife for confirmation. She dragged another oyster through a bowl of cocktail sauce, scarcely acknowledging her husband as she siphoned down her vodka. Both Jan and the bar where she sat were splattered with sauce. The bar tender had long since given up trying to clean up after her.

"Everybody else that's priced the job must think I don't know a damn thing about construction but I was responsible for a lot of it in the Army," Tom tilted his head proudly and continued. "You wouldn't believe the prices some of these contractors have given me. They're all crazy if they think they can gouge me out of my money just because they don't think I know nothin' about buildin'. Clovis is the only honest one of the bunch, and he knows I know my way around a job site. I know what I'm doin', am I right or wrong, Jan?"

With a sloppy grin, Jan zealously affirmed his declaration, "You tell him, Tom. We're going to build the *coshiest* little love *nesht* on Parker Avenue," she said, "I don't think *there'sh* a thing you can't do."

"Tom," Sam eyed him skeptically. "Are you sure you wanna do this?"

"Let me setcha straight. I was helpin' build bridges and puttin' up Army barracks when you were wet behind the ears. Am I right or wrong, Jan?"

Jan feigned a smile, tilted her head, then drooled into her cocktail sauce. "Tell him to mind *hish* own damn *bishnissh*, Tom. Tell him to go to hell."

Nature called. Jan thundered off her

weary bar stool and staggered toward the ladies room. She was five-foot-six and weighed
in at just under three hundred pounds. She
wore tight-fitting polyester pants and an un-
tucked blouse dangling loose at her mid-sec-
tion. The badly soiled blouse was pushed nearly
a foot from her chest by her profuse bosom. She
wore her bleached blonde hair rigidly plastered
in place with cheap, smelly hair spray.

Her disproportional skinny legs looked as
if she got much heavier, they would buckle right
at her knobby knees. Her bloated cheeks were
laced with purple veins, that, in spite of her
heavy make up, became more pronounced with
every vodka. Her overall appearance was reminiscent of the Tasmanian she-devil of cartoon
fame.

"Ain't she beautiful," Tom said as his fail-
ing eyes followed her away. When she disappeared into the ladies room, Sam turned back
toward Tom.

"If you're happy, I'm happy. But Tom. I
think you're making a mistake by not checking
out this Lark character."

The Yellow Pages were brimming with ad-
vertisers under the headings *Building Contractors* and *Contractors-General.* Although most

of the listings were for reputable businesses or individuals offering their services, many who called themselves "Contractors" or "Builders" did not aspire to excellence. Neither were they bubbling over with scruples.

Over the years Sam had seen many unwary property owners hooked by the sweet smell of low price. And many times the bad taste of poor quality lingered long after that sweet smell had dissipated. Competition among those in the building trade was fast and furious. And corners cut meant fatter purses for the unscrupulous.

"Don't trouble yourself over it, Sam," Tom said with a grin. "I know what I'm doin'. I can saw a board and swing a hammer with the best of em. Besides. You gotta get up pretty doggone early in the morning to pull one over on old Thomas C. Marshall."

A family of six was vacating a table right beside where Hat Man had set up and was making his music. Sam excused himself, grabbed the table and listened to Hat Man while waiting for Brit to finish work.

Hat Man was just starting his third set when Brit came to the table with an arm full of news papers, two oyster knives, saltine crackers, and several small containers of cocktail sauce. Hat Man smiled at Sam as Brit spread the news paper over the table and placed the condiments and knives on the paper.

Brit went to the kitchen and momentarily returned with two buckets of oysters and a hand-full of napkins. She placed the buckets on the table, sat down, and pulled her chair next to Sam's

"Look at the size of this one," Sam said, opening a giant oyster. He tried to hand it to Brit but she refused.

"You have it," she said. "If it's true what they say about them, you'd better eat your fill," she whispered. Her eyes beamed as she nibbled the end of her finger.

Before the end of Hat Man's set, Sam finished two buckets and ordered a third. Just as Gloria brought them to the table, Hat Man announced he was taking a short break. He turned down the microphone, pushed a Jimmy Buffet compact disk into his computer, then mindfully wiped down his guitar strings with a towel. After going to the bar, he brought his O'Doul's, to Brit's and Sam's table.

"Have a seat, mate," Brit motioned toward an empty chair. "I see you are still swilling that grog with no nectar."

"Yeah," Hat Man sighed. "I've been off the sauce for five years now. This stuff don't make me stupid and it don't taste too bad really. March thirty-first, huh?"

"That's the big day," Sam said, sipping his O.F.C and coke.

"After you do your best man thing, we want you and Charlie to play at our wedding party."

"Glad to. I'll set it up with Charlie. Where are you two going to do the deed?"

"Right here on the property, down by the water," Brit told him. "This is where we met so it's only fitting that we have the service here."

When time for Hat Man to go back to work, Brit and Sam went out on the deck. The sun was shining, the birds were singing, and the sky was blue. People dotted the sandy landscape flying kites, throwing Frisbees, and passing around footballs. Children were playing with their pails in the sand as lovers walked by them, hand in hand. Standing near the surf, and angler hooked a big one. Brit and Sam stood arm in arm, and watched the man fight to land his fish. It was a wonderful day to be in love.

The next two weeks passed quickly. Sam gave up the cabana and moved into Brit's condo. Every day he went to Clyde's job-site and checked the progress. Brit and Sam drove to Augusta and picked up Sam's old work truck from Clyde's warehouse where it had been in storage. Sam hired two laborers and notified Jerry of the starting date. He spent his evenings reviewing the plans and listing the material he would need. He also ate a lot of oysters. When the time came, he'd hit the ground running.

12

Monday morning, at seven-thirty, Sam and Jerry were standing at the drawing table in the job trailer when they heard foot steps. The distinct odor of boiled crabs quickly filled the room. Sam turned to find Mister Willie Washington and his nephew, Kareem, rambling toward them. Over the years Sam had employed Mister Willie for his labor all over the state.

Mister Willie was seventy-years old. He wasn't the fastest man alive with a pick and a shovel, but he worked steadily and never missed a beat. Sam trusted Mister Willie and he could always count on him.

Winter or summer, rain or shine, Mister Willie wore the same green Army jacket with deep pockets stuffed full of boiled crabs. Every day at ten o'clock break, at lunch, and again at three, he would find a spot to sit and eat them. Little piles of crab shells were always scattered about the job, telling of Mister Willie's whereabouts when he took a breather.

"Mornin' Mistah Sam. Sorry I'm late. I had to wait on dis boy to get his ass outa bed."

"Hey, Mister Willie," Sam shook his hand. "Great to see you. It's been a long time now."

"Yes suh, yes suh. Too long."

"Grab your shovels, and we'll get started. Here, keep these on your key ring," Sam threw Mister Willie a set of keys to the job trailer and tool room.

Sam rolled up the blue prints, put his architect's scale into his back pocket, and led his crew to the site of the main building. Using his scale, he mapped out the ditches, then marked the route on the ground with blue-powdered chalk.

"There you go," Sam said to Mister Willie. "The starting elevation is twelve inches below grade and I want the ditch to drop one-eighth inch per foot. You know what to do. Keep it between the lines."

"Yes suh, Mistah Sam, between da lines."

Sam left Mister Willie in charge of excavation and proceeded with Jerry to get what he needed to install the underground plumbing.

Kareem's given name was Nathanial Tyrone Green but he'd recently changed it. He believed the new one he'd chosen better reflected his African heritage. Kareem had been in and out of trouble ever since he was nine years old. He wore a black ball cap, with a big white X printed on the front of it, facing backwards on his head.

"Why you let dat white mutha-fucka talk to you da way he do?" said Kareem.

"What choo talkin' bout?" Mister Willie snapped, his eyes narrowing.

"He call you Mistah. Dat ain't nuthin' but shit. You ain't nuthin' but a nigga to him."

"How yo crack-ass brain come up with shit like dat? Fool. Sam Lewis don't look on me for no nigga!"

"How come you don't be doin' nuthin' but diggin' ditches?" Kareem asked arrogantly.

"Cause dat what I do...and I do it damn good. You ain't gwine see Mistah Sam down here fuckin' wid me. No...he respec me cause he know my woik gwine be right."

"Dat mutha-fucka don't give no shit bout you. He just want some Uncle Tom to do da shit he don't wanna do," Kareem pressed on.

"Look heah boy. Yo momma axe me to hep you. Now, don't be startin' yo shit. Where you think I got's da money to get yo crack-ass outa jail, Tyrone?"

"My name Kareem."

"I don't care nuthin' bout yo skreet name, boy. I axe Mistah Sam to bail you out. He ain't had to. He ain't had to send me no Amtrak ticket to Atlanna neither, back when I ain't had no woik. He ain't had to pay for me no hotel room, right next to his'n at da Holiday Inn, and feed me every night da whole time we was in Atlanna. He ain't had to give me no two-thousand dollar bonus when da job be over. He paid me good."

Kareem said nothing.

"And he ain't had to take me to Boomershine Chevrolet and hep me buy no car. Why, if it wadn't for Sam Lewis, dey was times you and yo momma woulda went to bed hungry. So da next time you call him a muthafucka I'm gwine slap you upside yo damn head wid dis shovel. Now, keep yo mouth shut and maybe you learn sump'm."

Mister Willie constructed a simple device to help him properly grade the ditch. He found a straight, eight-foot two-by-four, to use for a grade-board. He reached into his pocket and removed four pennies, stacked them together, and duct-taped them to the narrow edge of the board, midway down its length. He taped a two-foot aluminum level to the board with one end barely resting on the pennies, raising that end of the level a quarter inch above the board. With a marking pen he drew an arrow on the board in the direction the ditch should be dug.

By raising the level a quarter inch in its two-foot span, and keeping the bubble centered when grading, the desired eighth-inch per foot pitch would result. If elevation had been critical, Sam would have provided a ruby laser for Mister Willie to set the grade, but for that application a grade board would suffice.

Beside the trailer was a fenced yard with miles of hub and spigot, service weight, cast iron pipe stacked inside the fence. Several wooden crates filled with fittings of the same material sat next to the pipe. Sam instructed Jerry to start carrying down the ten-foot lengths of four-inch pipe and to lay them in a line by the ditch.

While Jerry struggled with the heavy pipe, Sam sorted through the crates and chose the fittings he would need. He returned to the tool room, located the propane tank, burner, ladle, and iron melting pot. He took the tools outside and put them in a wheel barrow along with fifty pounds of lead ingots and a package of oakum. The oakum consisted of thick strands of loosely twisted hemp and was used as the medium to pack cast iron plumbing joints. If Sam were using p.v.c. pipe and fittings, his job would have been easier, but Clyde was from the old school and insisted on using cast iron.

Sam rolled everything down to the work area and unloaded it all near the ditch. With Jerry watching every move, Sam lit the burner, filled the pot with lead, then went to his work. By then, Mister Willie and Kareem had graded nearly a hundred feet.

Sam measured off the batter board and drove a stake in the center of the ditch just behind where Mister Willie and Kareem were working. He measured again, drove another stake at the starting point, and pulled a tight nylon cord between the two stakes.

"It looks like you know what you're doing," Jerry commented, admiring Sam's prowess.

"I believe in pulling these strings, Jerry. When it's done right, you can run a hundred feet of pipe, look down one end, and see a perfectly round hole at the other."

Jerry and Sam put the pipe together in the ditch from stake to stake. With a plumb bob, Sam centered the pipe directly under the string, straight as an arrow. With his tools and a bag of oakum, he straddled the pipe and began making the first joint.

He looked into his tool bag for his yarning iron, wrapped a piece of oakum around the pipe, and with his iron, skillfully jammed the oakum into the fitting. He took a hammer, his packing iron, and tapped the oakum into proper compaction, following the full radius of the pipe. The procedure was repeated until the oakum was within an inch of the rim of the hub. Sam reached for his joint runner, a heat-proof rope with a metal clip, in preparation to pour the lead.

He stretched the runner around the pipe and clipped the ends together leaving a small opening at the top next to the joint. He made certain the runner was snug against the fitting so no lead could escape, then checked to see that the pipe was still properly aligned with the string.

"Bring me some soup, Jerry. And be careful."

Jerry went to the burner, dipped the ladle into the smoldering lead and brought it to Sam. The liquid was hot and bubbling when Jerry handed it to him. Sam poured the lead into the opening until the joint was full. After a few seconds, when the lead had sufficiently cooled, he removed the joint runner and chiseled away the excess lead. With his hammer and caulking iron, he scored the lead until the joint was positively sealed.

"That's all there is to it, Jerry," Sam stood from the ditch.

"After we make a few hundred more of these, we can take a vacation."

"I'm impressed by your expertise," said Jerry. "You make it look easy. How long did it take you to learn everything you need to know about plumbing?"

"I'm still learning."

At the end of the day, Sam felt good. A wise man once said the only real satisfaction a man can find in life is the good food he eats and a job well done. Sam was proud of the day's work, and he was hungry.

13

The next few weeks proved productive. Sam hired two more journeymen plumbers and their helpers out of Atlanta and everything was running smoothly. Jerry's value out-shined Sam's expectations. Jerry was happy in his work and wasn't bored because there was much to learn. At every juncture, Jerry took the ball and ran with it. Sam had only to show him once before he caught on. That was refreshing. There was someone willing to learn and worth the effort for Sam to teach him.

Jerry was amazed at the knowledge required to perform tasks that most people took for granted. Some of America's most brilliant minds made their living working in the construction business. Engineers and architects crowned the top of the industry. They directed the Master builders and tradesmen. In turn, the Masters directed the next level, journeymen plumbers, electricians, welders, carpenters, and so on.

Sam recalled the beginning of his career and related it to Jerry. The State of Georgia and every other state required plumbers, electricians, and heating and air conditioning contractors to be duly licensed for the same reason they licensed physicians: the public's health and safety depended on their expertise.

Every structure in a given area was connected to every other structure by a system of pipes. All similarly situated buildings were attached to sewers filled with every filthy thing flushed down the commode or spat into the sink. The sewer was home to every vile disease that threatened the human condition.

Sanitary plumbing separated structures

from the sewer and from each other by water seal traps. The trap on every plumbing fixture was filled with water and prevented gas exchange between buildings and the sewer system. The solidity of the trap's seal was insured against siphonage by a vent system.

If fixtures weren't properly trapped, an open line would have existed from the dwelling straight to the sewer, and an unhealthy condition would have been the result. Primitive cultures had little potable water. They bathed and defecated in the same water they drank. If not for the science of sanitary plumbing, Americans would have suffered the same plagues third-world countries endured. They would have been living in, and breathing the same atmosphere disease-ridden rats and roaches infested.

There was a standing joke about the simplicity of the plumbing trade: "The hot went on the left, the cold went on the right, and shit didn't flow up hill," but there was something more to it than that. Plumbers protected the health of the nation. Sam was a craftsman and an expert in his field with an educational equivalent to a Master's degree in the academic world.

At nineteen, he went to work for Rodney Pike, a plumbing and mechanical contractor in Macon, Georgia. Lester, the journeyman plumber he apprenticed under, was a strict task-master who demanded excellence in craftsmanship; he would settle for nothing less. After four years hard work and hours of study necessary to understand the theory, Sam passed his journeyman's test and was given his own jobs.

During the next four years, his studies continued and he worked in all phases of construction, simple single family residences to heavy industrial projects. Finally, confident in his knowledge and with his mentor's blessing, he was ready to take the state Master's exam.

One-sixty-six Pryor Street, Southwest, Atlanta, Georgia, was an address Sam never forgot. It was cold and foggy that February morning in 1980 when he went to take his test. While making his way through unfamiliar streets of downtown, he vaguely spotted a parking garage in the distance.

When he walked into the state examining facility, thirty-three hopefuls were standing about the lobby, code books in hands, waiting for the call to enter the auditorium. It looked like a family reunion as most recognized the other from previous attempts to run the gauntlet.

When the bell tolled, everyone left their code books at the door, as per decree of the examining board. The room's seating capacity was 150. To minimize cheating, the examinees were instructed to leave three chairs between them when taking their seats. The speaker directed his three assistants to pass out test booklets and computer-generated answer sheets with an ample supply of number two lead pencils.

The test was divided into two parts given over an eight-hour period with two ten-minute breaks and a half-hour for lunch, much like a plumber's work day. Part one consisted of a hundred questions covering plumbing fundamentals, technical subjects, mathematics, and basic sciences. The first few multiple choice questions were relatively simple but, as the morning wore on, the questions grew increasingly more technical.

Before morning break, everyone was cautioned not to discuss the exam, and informed that anyone not returning promptly at ten minutes after ten, would be locked out. After the break, twenty-nine returned to finish the test. Later, when lunch break was over, only seventeen remained.

The second half of the test not only demanded knowledge of technical aspects and theory but also necessitated skill of mechanical drawing, and aptitude to design and engineer

sanitary plumbing and water distribution systems in a multistory building.

The remaining seventeen men were given
a drawing, the size of a standard road map, pic-
turing a five-story structure and noting type and
location of all plumbing fixtures. The men were
instructed to fill in the blanks, as it were, by
drawing piping to all fixtures as well as including applicable valves, shock arrestors and back-
flow prevention devices. The five floors at and
above street level contained a hundred fixtures
in all.

The building included a basement with
thirty fixtures below the elevation of the sewer
main, necessitating the installation of a twin-
motor, sewage ejector, housed below ground in
an eight by eight-foot cylinder called a sump.

Even with all Sam's gathered knowledge,
he was rightly challenged by some of the intri-
cacies of the exam. It was imperative that the
Masters understood the seriousness of their
profession. The most formidable task of the
exam brought home the point with resounding
clarity. Sam was required to diagram a layout
for an autopsy room and make certain the
corpses bodily fluids couldn't contaminate the
building's main water supply system. The con-
sequences of a botched job were unthinkable.

After three o'clock break, eleven were left to complete the examination. It was nearly six weeks before Sam learned the result of his endeavor to join the ranks of select individuals with unrestricted license to practice the trade. Of the eleven men who finished the exam, five made the grade.

Sam and his crew poured the last subterranean joint three days prior to Brit's father's arrival. They'd have a few weeks to install the underground plumbing in the restaurant, salon and out buildings before starting the second phase of the first installation. The slab would be poured, the block work done, the framing complete, and the roof dried in before Sam would return to the main building.

14

That afternoon, Sam arrived at the Shipwreck and waited for Brit to finish her shift. He'd worked hard that day making sure everything was in order before calling for his inspection. It was happy hour and the place was crowded.

Sam spotted Tom Marshall sitting at the bar. Tom had his share of beer and was really on a roll. Tom's drunken wife sat next to him wobbling about on her stool. She was nearly asleep; her eyes were sunk deep into her fat.

"What happened to your ear, Tom?" Sam asked, noticing the big bandage.

"Caught it on a barbed wire fence."

"You don't have much luck, do you, buddy? How's everything coming along?" Sam asked, regarding Tom's remodeling endeavor.

"Couldn't be better, my boy," Tom said proudly, rearing back on his stool and pointing his finger.

"That Clovis Lark is slicker than owl shit. He's torn the roof off my house and he's gettin' ready to stand up the walls for the second floor."

"Where are you and Jan staying?"

"We're still livin' there. Yesiree, buddy, and it's savin' me a killin'. Clovis ripped off the roof without spillin' so much as a splinter into my cornflake bowl."

"You mean you're staying in the house during major renovation?" Sam asked, not sure he'd understood.

"That's what I'm tellin' ya. And that ain't the best part. Clovis is puttin' in the plumbin', he's puttin' in the lectrical, and he's puttin' in the heatin' and air conditionin'. He's savin' me a killin' I tell ya. A killin'!"

"Tom, I checked around. He doesn't have the licenses to do all that work."

"He don't need a license. It's my house and I got the right to put in my own plumbin', my own letrical, and my own air conditionin' long as it passes inspection. That's what Clovis says and that's what it says on my buildin' permit. It ain't lyin' really. I *am* overseein' everything. Clovis knows what he's doin'. I been watchin' him. Am I right or wrong, Jan?"

Jan picked her head off the bar and slobbered. "You tell him, Tom. *There'sh* nothing you can't do. You're my hero."

It was a thorn in Sam's side that non-licensed individuals, known as jacklegs in the construction industry, were allowed to compromise the public's health and safety. He would have belabored his displeasure with Tom but what was the point? After all, the old man's alcohol-soaked brain was fixated and encouraged by his rotund partner in marriage.

At 2:45 the following morning, the Marshalls were asleep. The weather office had predicted clear skies for the week, but Mother Nature planned differently. Within forty minutes she dumped three inches of rain on the Marshall's sheet rock ceiling. After the ceiling gave way, Jan lay next to her sleeping husband in a wet bed covered in slimy gypsum.

Two inches of water were on the floor and

more falling from the sky. Sparks flew about the room as electrical circuits went haywire. Pictures were ripped from walls and things were broken by crashing sheet rock.

Jan barely opened her eyes when she reached for her vodka. She unscrewed the cap and drank. She belched loudly, then drank again. Tom was still asleep when she slapped him hard on the small of his wet back.

"Get up and shut the window, you damned old fool. *Ish* rainin' in here."

15

Sam called for his inspection. He and his crew had capped off every opening in the building drain except the ten-foot riser pipe where they'd filled the system with water. Altogether Jerry counted 630 lead and oakum joints in the system. Jerry was pleased with himself and Sam was proud of him. Twenty-three of the joints were ones Jerry had made all by himself.

With flashlights, the crew closely examined every joint for leakage and found a problem with only seven. The leaks were easily corrected with a caulking iron, hammer, and a little elbow grease.

While waiting for the county inspector to

arrive, Sam, Jerry, and the rest of Sam's crew walked the job and checked everything one last time. The incoming water line supplying the building had been installed to exacting specifications. The installation was a four-inch service fabricated of ductile iron pipe, and stubbed into the mechanical room. The mechanical joint below grade was protected against blowout by a concrete thrust block. The concrete was poured behind the joint and against unexcavated earth, as per code.

The iron bodied gate valve, where the copper water main would one day attach, was securely bolted to the flange and tied to the mechanical joint with threaded steel rod. The service was hydrostatically pressurized to a hundred pounds per square inch and had held pressure overnight.

Sam was satisfied that he'd done the job to the best of his ability and even taped his business card to the main vent stack. That was the gauge Sam used to judge his own work. If he could sign his name to it, then he'd done the best he could; but the apprehension of his first inspection showed.

"You seem a little nervous, Sam," said Jerry.

"You can tell, huh. I always get this way

before an inspection."

Jerry shook his head and said, "Come on man. You do good work. Hell, I've been watching you work your buns off...going behind everybody, double checking everything, then checking it again." He gave Sam a pat on the back. "You got that much pride, buddy."

"I guess pride is a part of it. My grandfather always told me that if I'd strive for perfection, I'd always achieve excellence. But I don't care how good somebody is, they can always make a mistake."

Sam instinctively removed a torpedo level from his hip pocket and checked the degree of fall on a length of pipe. "Damn, Mister Willie is good," he said absently. Sam managed a weak smile as he returned the level to his pocket.

"I don't know a whole lot about the business, Sam, but from watching you I'd bet my boat the inspector is gonna sail through this like a midsummer breeze."

"I love your optimism, Jerry."

"C'mon. You ever fail an inspection?"

"Once," said Sam with a grimace. "And I never want to go through that again."

Jerry laughed a bit. "Are you telling me that not passing an inspection on the first go round bothers you that much?"

"No. I just remember Rodney Pike's face when he found out I'd failed my first inspection," Sam lit a cigarette. "I'd just got my journeyman's ticket and was working unsupervised for the first time. Rodney had given me a helper and bought me a brand new yellow *Chevy Luv* pick-up truck with a pipe rack and a nice set of tool bins.

"I'd just finished plumbing a house in a gated community in Macon called Lake Wildwood. There was a small drip on a drain fitting about thirty feet under the crawl space," Sam smiled and shook his head.

"It was too late to fix it because the inspector was on his way," Sam remembered how hard he'd worked to do his first job without a flaw. "Old man Ed Smith was the inspector. He'd been retired from plumbing ten years but he didn't miss a trick," Sam dropped his cigarette and snuffed it with his boot. "He could smell a leak like a hound dog. He crawled under the house with his level and flashlight and damned if he didn't go straight to it."

"And that's when he turned you down?" Jerry asked.

"Yeah. But that's wasn't the worst of it," Sam laughed again. "Rodney Pike was madder than a sack of hornets and there was hell to pay. He took me out behind the shop, over by the Coke machine, and let it fly. We all called him 'Boss Hog' because of his stern disposition."

"Did he hose you down and hang you out to dry?" asked Jerry.

"Not exactly. He told me if I *couldn't* do the job, he *would* find someone who could. He had a way of making you feel lower than a snail crawling through the Grand Canyon. But above all he taught me it's best to measure twice and to cut once. He taught me to cover my ass."

"Uh, huh...I can see that," Jerry said with a smile.

16

The county vehicle pulled off the road beside the job-site. After a few minutes, an African-American woman got out and walked toward the job carrying a clip-board. She wore short cropped hair, navy-blue pants, a white blouse, and gold ear rings. She stopped a workman and inquired where the plumber was. Sam watched as the man pointed him out, then the woman proceeded in Sam's and Jerry's direction.

"Are you the plumber?" she asked.

"Yes ma'am."

"I'm from the county," she said, shuffling through her papers.

"Yes ma'am. What can I do for you?"

"You called for a plumbing inspection, didn't you?"

"You're the plumbing inspector?" Sam asked.

"What did you expect, a man?" she countered.

"Well, not necessarily, I suppose. You just look a little over dressed for the occasion, that's all."

"Are all the drain lines filled with water?" she inquired dogmatically.

"Yep."

"Is everything put in right?" she asked, reaching for an inspection sticker.

"It's all right, according to code," Sam told her, now confounded.

The woman wrote something on a piece of paper, then signed her name to a green sticker. She handed the sticker to Sam and instructed him to place it on one of the stand pipes.

"I'm Shaneeka Holmes," she said and gave Sam a business card. "When you're ready for your next inspection, I'll need twenty-four hours notice."

"Wait a minute," said Sam. "Aren't you

even going to check the plans or look at the work?"

"I've got a heavy list of inspections to do. And it's your responsibility to make sure everything is in order."

"I can't believe this. I was told you people are lax around here but I *was* expecting something more than just a courier to bring out a sticker."

"Who do you think you are? Don't try to tell me how to do my job," she said.

"Look lady. I'm not telling you *how* to do your job. I'd just like to see you do it."

"Well, all right," Shaneeka said, snatching the sticker from Sam's hand. If you don't like the green sticker, see how you like this one."

Shaneeka stepped across the batter board and placed a red stop-work order on a soil stack, then haughtily approached Sam.

"I'll be back tomorrow," she said. "And this time, I'll bring the chief inspector. He'll go over this job with a fine tooth comb. And it better be right."

Shaneeka went to her car, cranked the engine, and punched the accelerator. The tires squealed and left a streak of rubber on the asphalt. Jerry was baffled.

"A little less thorough than I anticipated,"

he said. "Looks like things have changed since you last worked."

"Yeah," said Sam, shaking his head. "I guess they have."

After lunch, Sam spoke with the electrician on the project, Oliver Mathews. Oliver had been the electrical contractor on Clyde's job in Atlanta; Clyde considered him to be the best in the state. Oliver grew up in a housing project in the slums of Atlanta, but later his home was a five-bedroom split-level in Tucker. He was fifty-one years old and proud of his black heritage.

Though rooted in poverty, Oliver pulled himself up by his boot straps, worked hard, and determined that one day he and his family would have a better life. He started out digging ditches for an electrician and persevered until he learned the trade. Oliver put himself through college and worked until he obtained his degree in business administration. After graduation, he passed his Master Electrician's exam, then he was off and running.

Oliver and his wife, Cynthia, started their business on a shoe string, and in a relatively short time, they achieved an impressive degree of financial success. The business blossomed and grew to a corporate crew of 103 employees. Oliver owned fifty trucks, and the company generated gross annual revenues just shy of twenty million dollars. He was held in high regard by his business associates and his peers. He was judged "not by the color of his skin, but by the content of his character."

"I think I ticked off the inspector," Sam said after stopping at a junction box where Oliver was making some connections. Oliver checked everything once again, then closed the door to the box.

"So that's why Shaneeka peeled out of here like she did." Oliver shook his head. "You must have really struck a nerve."

"She didn't even look at the plans *or* the work. She just asked me a couple of questions, then handed me a green sticker. When I asked what was going on, she got up in arms and slapped a stop-work order on me."

"Well," Oliver cocked his head. "You said Clyde told you the inspectors around here aren't as tough as the ones in Atlanta."

"Yeah, but I did expect to see some display of knowledge about what she was inspecting or...*supposed* to be inspecting."

"That's the thing," said Oliver. "She doesn't have the knowledge to display."

"Then who the hell is gonna know if it's right or not?"

"You will, Sam. Just like I know about my end of it. That's why Clyde hired us."

"Sounds like you've worked in this county before," Sam lit a cigarette.

Oliver eyed Sam a moment. "Yeah, I have. I was sort of like you the first time. You know. I was proud of my work and I wanted somebody to at least acknowledge all the effort and experience that went into it."

"So now you just ride with the tide and go with the flow?"

"Don't have a choice. I just handle every job like my family is gonna be living in the place I'm wiring. When I'm satisfied the work is done right, I call for inspection. I sleep well."

"But how can the county hire people who don't know what they're doing?" Sam asked with an indignant tone.

"I used to ask myself that question. But I didn't like any of the answers I came up with. So I just do the best job I know how."

Sam shook his head slowly. "Someone once told me it's a good day when you learn something. I guess today is one of those *good* days."

"Uh, huh. Until Clyde finds out about the stop-work order," said Oliver with a grin.

"You think he's gonna hit the roof?" Sam

asked, knowing the answer.

"Yep," Oliver nodded. "Just before he goes through it."

17

"Hold back your brumbies, luv. You've done your best; that's what counts," Brit said, stroking Sam's hair.

"Well, maybe," said Sam with a sigh. "But Clyde doesn't see it that way. He's mad as hell. He was planning to pour concrete in three days and now he's being held up a day. He says I blew my cool and it's costing him time and money. He thinks I should have kept my mouth shut and went on about my business."

"Well, next time, don't stick your bib in. You know your work is done well. Just do your job and don't concern yourself over it."

"I'm not cut out that way, Brit. The whole thing bothers me. What if my work *wasn't* right? What if Oliver's work wasn't right? Faulty work-manship can be a disaster."

Sam sat up in the bed, eyed Brit candidly, and explained.

"Shaneeka was going to sign off on my work without even looking at it. Think about it, Brit. I've got gas lines running underground on that job. What if I didn't bother to test them for leakage? What if I'd left a slow leak and gas accumulated in sufficient quantity to become volatile? What if a spark from a thermostat or some other device ignited the gas and set off an explosion?" Sam shook his head. "The whole damn place and everybody in it would have been blown sky high."

Sam explained how something as seemingly innocent as condensate from an air conditioning system could be deadly. In 1976, an outbreak of 221 cases of pneumonia was associated with an American Legion convention at Philadelphia, Pennsylvania. It was determined that the bacterium, legionellosis, was the causative agent, hence the name Legionnaire's Disease. There was a fifteen to twenty percent mortality rate for persons who actually developed the pneumonia.

Legionellosis thrived in fresh water. The irresponsible disposal of condensate from a cooling tower at the convention resulted in the sickness and deaths of many people. Faulty workmanship and faulty inspections was no laughing matter and Sam was livid.

"That's one of the things I love about you Sam'o," Brit smiled. "You care about what's right. But you can't change the world. And you know what they say. When in Rome..."

"Yeah, well," Sam shook his head as he extinguished his cigarette. "And another thing," Sam continued. "Oliver told me the Chief Inspector doesn't know any more about plumbing than Shaneeka. And he's crazy to boot."

Chief Inspector Jeffery Andrews had recently been appointed to his job. He was insecure in his capacity because he believed his subordinates were plotting to usurp his position. He'd been diagnosed years before as a paranoid schizophrenic with suicidal tendencies. Lithium and Prozac kept him on a marginal keel, but when he felt good and got off his medication it was "Katy bar the door."

"Yeah, I guess I don't have much choice in the matter," said Sam. "You can't fight City Hall unless you've got the money to do it. But when this job is over, I want to move someplace else...someplace where they still have high standards. Any suggestions?"

"You've always said you'd like to see Brisbane. I don't think they'd put up with this sort of thing there."

"Yeah baby, let's do it. That would be fantastic. You can take me diving and show me the Great Reef."

"And we'll stroll through the Botanic Gardens then on to Mount Coot-tha," Brit's eyes sparkled. "You can see *all* of Brisbane from there. We'll bathe in Elebana Falls at Lamington Park, and stroll through the rain forest at Mount Tamborine! Oh, Sam'o, I love you so."

"And Fraser Island?" Sam asked, knowing Brit's kinship to it.

"Oh, yes! I'll surely take you there."

"And to Platypus Bay?"

Brit moved closer and held his face in her hands. She kissed his lips and rubbed her cheek on his. She looked away a moment, then came a placid smile.

"Sam'o, promise me something, will you? Promise you'll make love with me at the bay...there in the water, there in the moonlight."

With words so sweet, Brit painted the sea as the mysterious golden orb would slowly transcend the horizon and rise over the glossy stillness. The purest light would bathe them as they'd follow its path into the water. And when they'd hold one another, they'd absorb into their "Dreaming" and mingle with all creation: one with the universe. Then, when the loving was finished, the moon would complete its cycle and disappear into Platypus Bay.

"I do love you too, Brit. What a beautiful thought...what a wonderful person. Of course I promise."

Brit's voice was like music, soothing the savage breast. Her touch was a poultice, a potion for his soul. Sam's anxiety was fading and he finally felt he could sleep. He needed that. The next day would be stressful.

"Roll over luv," Brit said to him. "I'll give you a rub and you'll dream of your promise."

Sam turned onto his stomach and held his pillow while Brit kneaded his muscles and soothed his mind. He'd dreamed of Australia since he was a boy. Somehow he always knew he'd end up there. But he'd never imagined how marvelous it could be. He'd never believed there was someone like Brit. Sam's worries left him as she softly whispered her lullaby.

"Platypus Bay...Platypus Bay
The angels all come there to
kneel and to pray
Platypus Bay...Platypus Bay
They trouble the waters
for healing they say
Platypus Bay...Platypus Bay
Let us be one in eternity's play
Platypus Bay...Platypus Bay
Our souls will be cleansed then
we'll fly away"

As Sam drifted to sleep, he saw it clearly. They held one another, unashamed of their nakedness, as the tranquil waters washed the world away.

White doves hovered nigh
Bearing love sent from heaven.
And peace shone about them
Their souls they did fly.

18

The county vehicle rolled up just after eleven o'clock the following morning. Sam had just finished giving Mister Willie his instructions for his next project. Since the job had been shut down, Sam used the idle time to formulate a game plan for the next phase of underground work.

The chief inspector was sixty-one years old. He was tall and formidable looking but his demeanor reflected his apprehension. His hair was red but graying, his face was a mass of freckles, and his teeth were dingy yellow. As he approached, he cautiously scanned the job site.

"Are you Sam Lewis?" he asked with a disconcerted look.

"I am," Sam held out his hand.

"I'm Jeffery Andrews," the man said, refusing the hand shake. "I'm the chief inspector and I answer straight to the county's Director of Inspections. What seems to be the problem?" Andrews' eyes darted side to side.

"I called for an inspection and I didn't get one," Sam declared.

"Ms. Holmes said she tried to give you a sticker but you copped an attitude. She thinks you have a problem because she is a black woman."

"That's bullshit," Sam snapped. Andrews flinched.

"Listen," said Andrews, his eyes looked wilder as they hastened too and fro. "She's in training to take her state certification exam. It's required if she is to keep her job."

"If she passes her certification, does that make her a Master plumber?" Sam demanded

"No it does not, Mister Lewis," he said, growing weary of the inquisition. "It just gives her a general idea of what to look for."

"And she'll have a general idea about electrical and air conditioning?" Sam challenged.

"Correct."

"Well, I'd like to pose a thought to you, sir," Sam said bluntly, then he lit a cigarette. "I've done plumbing work from Maine to Florida.

All the inspectors I've ever known were masters of their damn trades." Andrews was troubled. Things hadn't been going well for him lately. He didn't know whether to advance or retreat.

"If you call for a plumbing inspection, you get a plumber," Sam pressed on. "If you call for an electrical, you get an electrician. I want to know how Ms. Holmes or anyone else can tell me if my work is right when they're not a Master of what I do?"

"I don't have an answer for that," Andrews was down to his last nerve and Sam was getting on it.

"Who does?" demanded Sam. "I want to know."

Andrews hesitated a moment then responded. "The Federal Government. It's called Affirmative Action. There's nothing I can do. My hands are tied," he said in an irritated tone. "If our department doesn't have so many blacks, so many women, so many whatever, then the county will lose Federal funds."

"It's really come to that?" Sam asked. "It really doesn't matter if anyone is qualified as long as they fit the racial-gender mold?"

"Like I said, Mister Lewis. My hands are tied."

"Is there *any* criteria these people *do* have to meet?"

"They have to have a high school diploma or equivalent, three years in a construction-related field, and a driver's license," Andrews said, knowing his answer wasn't what Sam wanted to hear.

"Ah, bullshit. A construction-related field," Sam said sarcastically. "That could mean three years experience mixing paint in a hardware store."

"Mister Lewis," Andrews said trying to suppress his irritation, "I didn't come all the way out here to talk politics. I came to give you your inspection sticker. Now, let's have a look."

Sam followed Andrews while he walked the job site. Andrews went to the water service, placed his hand on the heavy iron gate valve, and tried to shake it.

"Looks solid enough. What's the cement for?" Andrews asked, looking down at the concrete thrust block.

"It's in the specifications and it's required by code."

""Yeah...oh, yeah. That's right. Where is the pipe that you filled with water?""

Sam led him to the ten-foot riser pipe and watched him survey the installation. Andrews reached for the pipe and shook it also. A splash of water fell onto his hand.

"That's what I like to see...a stack full of water. Okay. Everything appears to be in order," Andrews peeled the back off the green sticker and placed it on the pipe.

"Are you satisfied now, Mister Lewis?"

Sam knew when he was licked. He thought of the thousands of dollars Clyde had paid to the City of Tybee for his building permit. Tybee, in turn, had contracted with the county for their inspection services. Sam was beside himself.

"Well, Mister Andrews, I guess I just didn't understand the program. Tell Ms. Holmes I'm sorry if I offended her."

"She'll get over it. We all have our jobs to do. Let's just try to get along. And please, Mister Lewis, try to show Ms. Holmes the respect she deserves. The last thing I need is for her to holler discrimination."

"I'll do that, Mister Andrews. I certainly will. And say, by the way. What did you do before *you* became an inspector?"

"I drove a dump truck for thirty years. Why do you ask?"

"No reason, Mister Andrews," Sam shook his head. "I was just curious, that's all."

19

"Try and get some sleep, honey," Sam did all he could to soothe Brit as she tossed restlessly in bed. He rubbed her back and gently stroked her hair. It had been two hours since she first closed her eyes. The next day was Saturday, the day her father was to arrive.

Sam pulled on his sweat pants, went to the kitchen, and made a cup of herbal tea for Brit. She sat up, propped her pillow against the head board, leaned back, and relished the aroma rising from her cup.

"There now," Sam said, "that should take the edge off."

"Thank you," Brit breathed after sipping the brew. "Nothing like a hot spot of *Sweet Dreams* to get you through the night."

"It'll be all right, Brit. Ninety percent of the things we worry about never happen."

"I know," she said and squeezed Sam's hand. "It's just that I know how daddy can be."

"Just try to relax. Everything will be fine. I've got that feeling."

Brit finished her tea and turned out the light. Sam continued rubbing her as he softly hummed *Into the Mystic*. In a short time her breathing became shallow and regular, and Sam finally heard a little snore.

20

The hour's drive from Tybee to the airport was tense. Brit said little along the way. Instead, she suffered through the fan-tods, biting her nails, fiddling with her hair, and shuffling about in her seat. She'd spoken with her father just hours before but still had gleaned no clue of his mood. She'd prayed Sam's and Wilton's first meeting would be convivial but the tone in Wilton's voice was a mystery. Sam tried to keep his eyes on the road, and the big station-wagon between the lines but Brit's nervousness precluded his ability to properly do either.

Savannah International was lively when they arrived. It was 3:45 P.M., when the sleek Gulfstream IV touched down leaving a puff of rubber smoke in its wake. The shrill pitch of twin turbo-jets grew louder as the aircraft taxied off runway three-six and came to a halt on the tarmac at Savannah Aviation.

The plane left Brisbane Wednesday morning, refueled in Samoa, then landed on the Island of Hawaii for a service check and a chance for Wilton to visit a colleague at the University there. An airline, even Quantas, wouldn't have been nearly so accommodating. It was worth the expense.

When Wilton landed in Los Angeles, he dropped off his cargo, a pair of mated Koalas, the Brisbane zoo was trading for two unrelated Siberian, long-haired tiger cubs. Wilton was curator of the zoo and hoped to breed the cubs when they matured. He would pick them up on his return flight. Before take-off from Los Angeles International, the pilot filed a flight plan, and Wilton called Brit to let her know his expected time of arrival.

Wilton stepped off the airplane into balmy weather, not much different than the weather he'd left behind in Brisbane. He was a big man, nearly bald, with that same tropical tan Brit wore. When he smiled at her, his perfect teeth left no doubt that he was her father. After Wilton's and Brit's emotional embrace, Brit took Sam by the arm.

"Daddy, this is Sam."

Wilton scrutinized him a long while. To Brit and Sam, it seemed a small eternity. Wilton looked him up then looked him down. His lips were clinched as he slowly nodded his head.

"So," said Wilton with a voice that sounded like thunder. "You are the bloke who wishes to marry my daughter, eh?"

"Pleased to meet you, sir," Sam smiled and cautiously extended his hand.

Brit was troubled when Wilton did not readily accept the handshake, and she was aghast when he suddenly grabbed Sam's hand, pulled him off balance, then gave him a grand Aussie style bear hug that lifted Sam off his feet.

Sam backed up a step and reclaimed his breath. Wilton laughed, held his hand toward Sam and said, "G'day, Sam'o, It's a pleasure to finally put a face with the name."

Brit stood watching, nearly catatonic, not just over the bear hug but because her father called him Sam'o. The connotation struck her imagination. What had her father been about doing?

"You look as if you've seen a ghost," Wilton said to Brit with his omniscient smile. "I have a number of friends here in the colonies, dear Brittany, and one much closer than you know."

"You're fair dinkum, mate," he said, nodding at Sam. "I've known about you from the start...from the very first Bloody Mary my little girl ever brought you."

Brit glanced at Sam then back at her father. "Someone has been spying on us?" she asked.

"I wouldn't call him a spy," said Wilton. "I prefer to think of him as your guardian angel. The world can be a nasty place. I couldn't very well let you go out into it without someone watching over you."

"But why were you so vague when we spoke on the telly?" Brit asked.

"I thought the news might be a nice surprise."

"Surprise is an understatement," Brit hugged her father again but this time tears of relief welled in her eyes.

"There, now luv," said Wilton as he patted his daughter's back. "Forgive me if I've upset you."

"I'm not upset, daddy," she dried her eyes. "I just wanted so much for you to welcome Sam'o into the family."

"Then you have your wish. Welcome to the family, Sam'o. Now, let's be off," he said decisively. "I'm ready to visit the island."

Wilton got his luggage and the three made their way to the car. After Brit and Sam digested the "surprise," their tension eased appreciably. The ride back to Tybee was considerably more relaxed than the one to the airport. Sam found Wilton intriguing and Wilton confirmed all he'd been told of Sam. Brit was coming back around to her usual self and everyone was fairly comfortable.

21

After arriving at the Beach Resort, Brit and Sam showed Wilton around. Later, at Wilton's request, the three headed for the Shipwreck. Unbeknownst to Sam and Brit, he'd already made arrangements to lease the cabana for the duration of his visit.

It was nearly dark when the three arrived. As usual, Hat Man was providing the entertainment. Sam led the way through the Shipwreck's northern door with Brit and Wilton close behind. The place was alive with regulars and an array of weekend guests. Immediately ahead of them, leaning his back against the bar, was Jerry Kirbo. He sported a wide grin that broadened when he saw Wilton.

"Happy Saturday, Wilt'o," he roared.

"Happy Saturday to you, Jerr'o, old bean." Wilton quickly approached Jerry, lifted him up, and gave him the same rib-crushing bear hug he'd bestowed on Sam earlier that afternoon. "Gotten yourself a new pair of glasses I see. Same tint. Different style."

"Jerry!" Brit said to Sam. "Well, I never..."

"I never would have either," Sam said reaching for her hand. "C'mon baby, let's go have a drink."

For nearly half an hour, Brit and Sam sat on the other side of the bar watching Wilton and Jerry catch up. Their friendship predated the evacuation of Saigon.

The Australian and American governments had worked covertly then. Jerry was the American team leader, and Wilton was the Australian counterpart. They'd looked the devil in the eye and served their countries in ways the public would never know. Their ties were strong; their mutual loyalty was beyond question.

After their conversation, Wilton found Brit and Sam sitting on the other side of the bar by the waitress station. He saw the perplexity on Brit's face as he approached. An explanation was long overdue. Hat Man was playing a slow one, so Wilton took the opportunity to have a little time with his daughter.

"Care for a dance, Brittany," he said with an amiable smile.

Brit took her father's hand and he escorted her to the dance floor at the south end of the Shipwreck. While Brit and Wilton were having their dance, Sam joined Jerry at the bar. Sam ordered an O.F.C. *without* the Coke.

"Jerry, I thought you and I were supposed to be friends."

"That we are."

Sam finished off the drink and ordered another. "Friends don't bullshit friends," said Sam.

"What I did wasn't bullshit," Jerry motioned for Gloria to bring him another Miller Lite. "Wilton and I go way back," he continued. "We did a lot of drinking together. We did a lot of things our governments don't want us talking about. And more than once we nearly died in little countries most people never heard of."

"C.I.A?" Sam asked as Gloria slid the straight whiskey and the Miller Lite in front of them.

"Not even the C.I.A. knew about us."

Sam took a small sip and looked back at Jerry. "Well, it seems your reports to Wilton about me were favorable."

"Let's get this straight right now, Sam, so there's no misunderstanding. You are a new friend. Wilton is an old one. I knew you before Brittany came to Tybee. I liked you then and I like you now. When Wilton found out Brittany had come here, he asked me to look after her. Any 'reports' as you say, were strictly about Brittany's welfare."

"But you told him about me," Sam lit a cigarette. He said you..."

"Yes, I did."

"Well, what you told him must have been good. He says I'm 'fair dinkum'. I guess that means he thinks I'm all right."

"I believe that's a true statement," said Jerry before taking another swallow of his beer.

"Just for the hell of it," said Sam, swirling his drink around in his glass, "how would Wilton have reacted if you told him you didn't care for me?"

"You have to understand," said Jerry. "Wilton Hayes has to see things for himself. I told him you were good for Brittany but he still had to look you in the eye. It would have been the same if I told him you were bad for her."

"Well, whatever. I'm glad you thought I was a good guy."

"Me too, Sam. I would have been sad-dened to see you end up like Jimmy Nesbit."

Sam stopped cold as he was lifting his glass for another sip. "Whoa! Are you saying what I think you're saying?"

"What I'm saying is this. You're sitting here having a drink. Wilton is over there danc-ing with his daughter. All he ever wanted was for Brittany to be happy. She's happy. Very happy. Right now you are doing what is most important. You're making her proud. Always make her proud and you'll never go wrong. Happy Saturday, Sam." Jerry finished his beer, rose from the bar, and took his exit. He caught a glimpse of Wilton out of the corner of his eye and waved as he left.

Wilton and Brit finished their dance, then walked Sam's way. Sam gave Wilton a knowing nod and held his arms out for Brit. She came to him, laid her face against his and whispered, "I love you, Sam'o...I'll always love you." Nothing of it was ever spoken again. But the deal was sealed, and as far as Sam was concerned, it was chiseled in stone.

After Hat Man's second set, Brit, Wilton, and Sam had a bite to eat then headed for Doc's Bar.

22

Doc's Bar on Tybee's world-famous Tybrisa Street was established in 1948 and, like the Shipwreck, was a popular watering hole for many locals as well as a throng of tourists. The atmosphere was always relaxed and the staff was friendly and happy to be of service.

To the left of the entry way, the bar ran twenty feet before stopping just short of the kitchen, where an old hippie named Wizard worked his magic. Wizard kept his silver hair braided and it hung down his back nearly to his belt. His thick mustache grew past his chin like walrus tusks. He didn't talk much but he always wore an illegal smile as his brain was well smoked and pickled.

To the right of the entry way was a small stage where Charlie Sherrill worked *his* magic. Directly beside the stage was a booth he called the percussion table where Charlie kept an ensemble of easily played instruments: tambourines, maracas, bongos, and an afuche. Anyone who could keep time with the music was invited to join the show. Sam, Brit, and her father were lucky that night, the percussion table was theirs.

Charlie was not only a master of the tenor saxophone, alto sax, soprano sax and flute, he was also a gifted singer-song-writer. He was middle-aged and wore a thick black beard and mustache. His dark eyes were clear, honest, and mirrored the beauty of his music. The crowd stood in awe while he played with the genius of instrumental greats. Pete Fountain and Kenny G. had nothing on Charlie. He performed naturally, as music was his second nature. His instrument was an extension of himself, and he commanded it easily as one might order a hand to raise a glass or tip a hat.

Invariably, during Charlie's performance, someone would ask how he made it look so simple. The answer was always the same: swift, direct, and sincere. "God gives us our gifts and our talents and the music for us all."

Charlie was a friend to Brit and Sam from the beginning. When he learned of their marriage plans his heart sang and moved him to write a haunting love song for them, *Saxophone For Baby*. The song was to be included in his soon-to-be released compact disk, *Palm Street*. When he played it that night, Brit accompanied on the tambourine, Sam the bongos, and Wilton rattled the afuchi. Seeing his daughter finally happy and so vivacious brought much joy and laughter to Wilton Hayes.

After the first set, a parade of appreciative fans came to the stage and thanked Charlie for his dazzling performance. When they all returned to their seats, he came off the stage to the percussion table. As always, he was pleasant and reserved.

"You must be Brittany's dad," he said, shaking Wilton's hand.

"That'd be me, mate. Thanks for the concert," said Wilton, sliding a twenty dollar bill into the tip jar. "When I return to Oz, I'll ship you a didgeridoo."

"That's one instrument I've yet to master," Charlie laughed.

"Shouldn't take long. Your bonzer blowing will soon land you with the tall poppies," Wilton smiled. Charlie looked puzzled.

"Daddy said you play so well, it won't be long before you'll become very successful," Brit smiled.

"Thank you sir," Charlie was flattered. "I just try to give it my all," he said. "A couple of years ago I was lucky enough to be one of the opening acts when Ray Charles came to Savannah. After the show, he took me aside and told me not to worry about the money. He said if I pursue my music for the pure art of it, then the money will come. That's what I try to do. I won't cheat the gift."

"Say, Brittany, Sam. Randy and I have rearranged our schedules and we're all set to play at your wedding."

"Ripper, mate!" said Brit. "We want you to play *Saxophone For Baby* for our first dance, after we take our vows."

"That means more to me than you guys

will ever know. I'd be honored. Whup, check the time," Charlie said, looking at his watch. "Gotta get back to work."

After the next set, Wilton was ready to call it a night. He'd downed a few lagers and was feeling no pain. It had been a long day and the thought of ocean waves pounding the sea wall behind the cabana was more than inviting. Brit was off work the next day and she planned to spend it with her father.

23

The next morning, before picking up Wilton for a tour of the lighthouse, Brit stopped by Sam's job-site. Sam was talking with Mister Willie when she arrived. Brit had heard many good things about Mister Willie and was looking forward to meeting him. She was aglow when she walked their way.

"Ain't she something, Mister Willie," Sam said as she approached.

"She sho is. She da prettiest white woman I ever seen. She look like a movie star."

Sam placed his arm on Mister Willie's shoulder and said, "Mister Willie, this is Brittany." Sam swelled with pride.

Mister Willie removed his hat and smiled. "I sho is glad to meet you, Miss Brittany. You all Mistah Sam talk about."

"Top of the morning to you mate, it's a pleasure," Brit said, reaching for Mister Willie's callused hand. Mister Willie wiped his hand on his jacket before giving it to her.

"He crazy bout you. I been knowin' Mistah Sam a long time, and I ain't never seen him so happy."

"Lovely for you to say so, Mister Willie. Sam'o tells me you're fair dinkum yourself. You will be attending our wedding, I trust."

"Mistah Sam *know* I gone be dare. I gone be dare wid bells on."

When Sam walked Brit to her station wagon she told him how happy she was to have the opportunity to visit with her father. She hadn't spent time alone with him in well over a year. She was so excited. She wanted to take him to dinner at the Hunter House that night and Sam readily agreed. Sam stood beside her car and kissed her good-bye.

"I won't be seeing you again until this evening, luv. What will you do for lunch?"

"I don't know, I'll get by. Maybe I'll try and talk Mister Willie out of some crabs," Sam grinned.

"Charming fellow, Mister Willie. But you know, I scarcely understood a word that he said."

Brit drove away and Sam resumed his conversation with Mister Willie. Sam had a good laugh when he learned Mister Willie and Brit had something in common.

"You know, Mistah Sam, Miss Brittany a fine lady, but I don't hardly understand nuthin' she say."

24

When Brit arrived at the DeSoto, Wilton was not in the cabana waiting for her, nor was he in the Shipwreck. She went out the eastern door and up the ramp to the tiki bar. A feeling strangely akin to deja vu came over her when she found him sitting in the same chair where she'd served Sam his drink so many mornings before.

Wilton's feet were propped on the bench, and he stared introspectively over the ocean as he sipped his Bloody Mary. His face shone gentle radiance when Brit touched his shoulder.

"Good morning, daddy, did you sleep well?"

"Wonderfully peaceful here, luv. I slept

like Van Winkle. I was sitting here lost in the sea," Wilton said, rising from his chair. "Let's get a move on. I want to climb the tower."

The parking lot was crowded at the lighthouse and museum when Brit and her father arrived. Wilton was a history buff and fascinated by everything southern. As they ascended the 178 spiral steps leading to the light chamber, Wilton read a brochure explaining the history of the Tybee Light Station.

In 1733, General James Oglethorpe, founder of the British colony in Georgia, ordered construction of the first lighthouse on Tybee Island. When completed in 1736, the wooden structure stood ninety-feet tall and was said to have been the tallest building of its kind in all the colonies.

The general realized the need for building the lighthouse to illuminate the mouth of the Savannah river, but failed to consider the eroding nature of the Atlantic Ocean. When it became apparent the sea would reclaim its own, he ordered another lighthouse built farther from the water. In 1741, just after construction began on the new one, the first one washed away. By March of 1742, the new stone and wood structure was completed.

Much the best building of its kind in

America, General Oglethorpe boasted. But as
it happened, the general didn't take the hint
from the stormy Atlantic and built the second
one too close to the water as well. By 1768, a
third one had to be built farther inland and
wasn't completed until 1773. The third Tybee
Light stood 100 feet tall and was made of brick
with interior wooden stairs and landings. Giant candles and large metal discs first illuminated the lantern room but later sixteen whale
oil lamps were used.

An eight-foot, Second Order Fresnal lens
made of molded prisms was installed in the lantern room in 1857. The lens magnified the light
source so well that only one whale oil lamp was
needed to guide the maritime vessels.

In 1861, Confederate volunteers burned
the wooden stairs and landings to prevent Union
troops from making use of the facility. After
Union forces captured Tybee Island, they re-
built the stairs and landings in order to keep
an eye on Confederate forces holding out in Fort
Pulaski, just up the Savannah River.

By 1866, a new fire-proof lighthouse
made of brick with cast iron stairs and landings, was authorized. The lower sixty feet of
the old light house, with its twelve-foot-thick
brick walls was used as a foundation for the

fourth Tybee Light. Ninety-four feet were added to the foundation making the new structure rise 154 feet into the Tybee sky. A nine-foot, First Order Fresnel lens sent a beacon of light nearly twenty miles out into the Atlantic. As many as three lighthouse keepers maintained the lamp but the advent of electricity negated the need for them.

After Brit and Wilton reached the light chamber, Brit was surprised the light bulb was no bigger than a liter bottle of soda-pop.

"Sometimes big things come in small packages," Brit said, opening the door to the observation deck.

They stepped out onto the deck that circumvented the light house just below the light chamber. They were at once overwhelmed by the wonder and beauty. A panoramic vista of the Georgia and South Carolina coast lines nearly took their breath away. Off to the west, the view of the Talmadge Memorial Bridge connecting the mainland of Savannah to Hutchison Island was postcard perfect.

Moving counter clock-wise around the tower, a spectacular scene of the little town of Tybee Island sprawled before them. To the north, Hilton Head Island seemed closer than when observed from Brit's and Sam's deck back at the Beach Resort.

Brit and Wilton could clearly see Sam's job-site and Wilton's binoculars figuratively transported them there. Brit watched construction workers carrying out their respective tasks. She anxiously scanned the area hoping to catch a glimpse of Sam.

"You don't like being away from him, do you, Brittany?" Wilton asked.

"I'm never away from him, daddy...even when we're separated," she said sincerely, then faced her father. "I love him dearly."

Apart from reasons obvious to him, Wilton was curious why Sam unequivocally won his daughter's devotion. He'd wondered about it ever since he first learned of Brit's affinity for Sam. Now, with ardor reflected in her eyes, the question begged an answer.

"It's his heart," Brit said with simplicity. "He's gentle. And he's kind," she looked into cottony white clouds that floated in a vast expanse of cobalt blue sky and explained.

Sam's parents were killed in an automobile accident when he was three years old. Fortunately, his maternal grandparents were there for him, and he grew under their loving guidance. It was a blessing.

Sam's sister suffered mental retardation

from birth, which in a tragic way, was a blessing for Sam as well. Growing up, Sam was Sissy's companion, protector, and defender. Her affliction taught him patience and understanding for those less fortunate. Sam taught her to tie her shoes and to brush her teeth, though she did neither very well.

After their grandparents passed away, Sissy was placed in a personal care home where five other afflicted people became her new family. Sam had taken Brit to Macon twice to visit Sissy there. Brit was moved by Sissy's love for her brother.

"Sam'o and I drove to Macon one day so I could meet Sissy," Brit told her father. "She's the cutest little thing, daddy. She's only four-foot-ten with strawberry hair and the same blue eyes as Sam'o. She was so excited to see him. When she ran toward him, put her arms around him and buried her head on his chest, I couldn't help but cry.

"We brought her from the home to a Japanese steak house. Sam said she'd always loved her shrimp, and that day she surely ate her fill."

Brit told Wilton that Sissy had never been to a Japanese steak house before. Sissy was greatly entertained that afternoon. The chef cooked their meals on a griddle right at their table, and Sissy was thrilled at being the center of attention. Brit watched as Sam helped her with her plate, wiped her spills, and doted over her like a mother hen. Brit saw Sam's heart through the eyes of his little sister.

"Tell me about his grandparents," said Wilton.

Brit told her father what she knew of Charles and Elizabeth Brinkman. "His grandfather was a wonderful man and a gentle man. He was an independent grocer in Macon. He was patient, and kind. Sam'o is his living legacy."

Sam revered him. Many times Sam had told Brit if he could ever be half the man his grandfather was, he would have achieved magnanimity. Charles was generous, slow to anger, and quick to reprove.

Growing up, Sam worked at Brinkman's Food Store from the time he was old enough to get his work permit. He learned the work ethic and the value of a dollar when he was very young. Charles taught him determination and perseverance. "Can't never could," he instructed Sam, "but I'll try always gets by." Much of what Samuel Quincey Lewis was, Brit attributed to

Charles Brinkman.

"And his grandmother?" Wilton asked.

"She was quite the matriarch. She put the fear of God into Sam'o when he was very young. He's told me so many stories about his childhood...he keeps me in stitches with them. Oh! I just remembered a jolly one," Brit laughed. "It was about a Playboy magazine he'd stolen from a corner shop," she explained.

Sam was ten years old when his grandmother caught him with it. Her instrument of correction was a fly swatter, and that day, she nearly wore it out on his behind.

"And what's so funny, daddy, Elizabeth didn't stop there. She told him she intended to put him into reform school where they'd beat him with an electric whip. She let him stew over that a few days until she was certain he'd truly repented," Brit looked curiously at her father.

"I suppose with today's line of thinking, that would be considered child abuse. But Sam'o is thankful for it. He said it really did the trick. After that, he never stole so much as second base."

"I'm very pleased," Wilton said to Brit. "And I'm satisfied you've made the right decision. I'm very happy for you."

"Thank you, daddy. That's the best wedding gift anyone could give me."

After a final look around the observation
deck, Brit and Wilton descended the tower and
drove to the new pier and pavilion at the south
end of the island. They bought hot dogs and
Cokes at the concession stand, then spent the
afternoon visiting the shops on Tybrisa Street.

Brit took her father to the amusement
park for a ride on the Ferris wheel so he could
catch a view of the island from a different angle.
She made certain the operator let them sit in
the blue gondola. The first time Sam ever kissed
Brit, they were sitting in the blue gondola high
atop the wheel. Brit had all she'd ever wanted.
And it was wonderful to be alive.

25

It was five minutes before nine o'clock that
night when the trio pulled into the Hunter House
parking lot. John Hunter had purchased the old
place some years back, and over time, made it
into a quaint bed and breakfast inn. The old inn
was charming and antebellum. Artifacts that
John discovered after he bought the house hung
tastefully on the walls throughout every room.

The high ceiling and brass chandelier graced lavish wall paper in the foyer. The house was painted deep blue and was surrounded by a huge porch. The tin roof was supported by red brick columns. Antique rocking chairs were positioned around the porch next to dimly lit tables. Through the leaded-glass, mahogany entrance door was a roll top desk and a stool where John sat every night and greeted his guests.

"Hey Sammy," John smiled as everyone came through the door. "I've got your favorite table waiting on you, and I took the liberty of chilling a bottle of Vouvray. I heard the good news, when's the big day?"

"March thirty-first," Sam responded. "John, I want you to meet Wilton Hayes, Brittany's father?"

"It's a pleasure, sir," John said, shaking Wilton's hand.

"Hello, mate. My daughter and Sam'o have told me wonderful things about your restaurant. Perhaps, if you're available, we'll employ your services to cater the wedding," said Wilton.

"You bet," John smiled and winked. "I'm flattered. We do our best."

John was nearly fifty with silver hair and a mustache. He was a handsome man with a dark tan and a pleasing smile. He picked up three menus and led the way to the dining room. He sat the party at the table that was decorated with fine linen cloth. A vase containing a half dozen pink carnations was its center piece. While everyone was getting comfortable and discussing what they might have for supper, Espy Geissler, the co-owner of the establishment brought them the Vouvray.

Espy was a fine fellow. He was forty-something and chef extraordinaire. He usually wore baggy *Chef's Gear* with brightly colored peppers against a dark field of fabric. Sometimes there were mushrooms, onions, or tomatoes printed on his trousers and the colors were always in sharp contrast. His jacket was traditionally white and his white chef's hat sat high atop his head.

Espy was happy in his work, doing what he loved. He always tried to make the dish he was preparing just a little better than the last one he'd made. And after a lifetime of trying, his cuisine approached perfection.

"Sam, Brittany, congratulations are in order, enjoy this with our compliments," Espy said with a warm smile. He uncorked the frosty bottle and filled their glasses.

"Thank you very much," said Sam. "Espy,

I'd like you to meet Brittany's father, Wilton Hayes."

"Glad to meet you, sir," said Espy.

"The pleasure is all mine, mate," Wilton shook his hand. "I'm looking forward to sampling your edibles, but I'm bound to tell you. Sam's and Brittany's description of them will be a difficult act to follow."

"What's good tonight, my friend?" Sam asked him, knowing the answer.

"It's all good," responded Espy. "Your waitress will be here directly and explain all of our specials tonight. Enjoy your meals."

Presently, the waitress arrived, introduced herself, then described in scrumptious, mouth watering detail, the culinary delights that were there just for the asking at a modest price. They ordered their food and enjoyed the wine and conversation, while awaiting dinner. The taste sensation that the Hunter House was noted for providing was legendary and that night Wilton was not disappointed. And there was no doubt. He'd found a caterer. After a splendid meal of grilled seafood with mixed vegetables topped off by a slice of home-made key lime pie, Brit and Sam brought Wilton back to the Shipwreck. Wilton invited them in for a drink but the next day was a work day and Sam had much to do.

26

The following morning Sam and Jerry arrived at the job-site ready to roll. Mister Willie's car wasn't there, which gave Sam cause for concern. Every day Mister Willie arrived early, opened the job trailer, made coffee, and laid out the tools for the day's work.

As Sam slid the key into the door lock, Mister Willie's car came sliding sideways in the sand beside the trailer. The trunk vibrated and the trailer windows rattled from the loud and steady boom-boom emitting from Kareem's ghetto blaster. Mister Willie always drove cautiously, listened to gospel music, and babied his old Chevrolet he'd bought from Boomershine.

In a moment, Kareem got out of the car and strutted toward Sam and Jerry. Kareem was arrogant and wore his chip squarely on his shoulder beneath his Malcolm X cap.

"Where is Mister Willie?" Sam demanded.

"Willie sick. I be yo *H.N.I.C.* today."

"What?" snapped Sam.

"You know. Yo head nigga in charge," Kareem spat on the ground.

"What in the hell are you talking about? What's wrong with Mister Willie!?"

"Ain't nuthin' much. He got a touch o da

flu. Da's all. Everything gone be all right. You got choo a good nigga here."

That's it, thought Sam. Sam took a few seconds to collect his thoughts then turned to Jerry.

"Jerry, would you excuse us a minute?"

"All right," said Jerry. "If you need me, I'll be right around the corner."

Jerry turned and walked away. As soon as he was out of sight, Sam eyed Kareem intently. He walked down the steps as Kareem watched with caution. Kareem held his ground as Sam approached.

"What choo doin'?" said Kareem as Sam stood inches from him.

"We're going to put an end to this here and now, Kareem."

"Get out my face, mutha-fucka!" Kareem shouted and jabbed his finger into Sam's chest.

Sam shoved him hard, and slammed his back against the job trailer. Kareem lunged for Sam. Sam grabbed him by his shirt, spun him around, and threw him into the trailer harder than before. Kareem's eyes widened and rolled back in his head. Sam took a quick step toward him and Kareem winced.

"No Mistah Sam! I don't wanna fight."

"Then what do you want to do, you little

prick? If it weren't for your uncle I'd throw your ass off this job-site in a city second. What the hell is your problem, anyway?"

"I tired of doin' nigga woik like Willie do. Willie been a nigga all his life. Always will be. Black peoples like me and Willie ain't got a chance."

Sam walked slowly toward Kareem, squatted down beside him, and lit a cigarette. He took a long draw, looked at the ground, then looked back at Kareem. He exhaled, blew the smoke just over Kareem's head, then softly spoke.

"Get off it, Kareem. You don't deserve to be the same color as your uncle. The next time you call him a nigger, I'm gonna skin you alive and you'll be rosy red. Then what's your excuse gonna be? Are you listening to me, Kareem?"

Kareem looked at Sam, nodded his head, but said nothing.

"So, you think digging ditches is nigger work, huh?"

"Well," said Kareem. "What choo call it?"

"A starting point." Sam took another draw off his cigarette and thought a moment. "You don't know your uncle very well, do you?"

"What choo talkin' bout?" said Kareem

with a sneer. I knows Willie all my life."

"Then you should know he enjoys what he does. He could have been anything he wanted to be, still can. But ditch grading is second nature to him. He says his work frees his mind to think about more important things. I respect him for that."

"Huh," said Kareem. "Da only way we black peoples gets respec be to fight fo it. You ever see da movie, Malcom X?"

"No," said Sam, looking at Kareem's cap. "But I did read the hat. You think you've got it all figured out, don't you, Kareem? You think you know how it was. But you don't. You weren't there. I was."

"What choo talkin' bout?"

"When I was a small boy your uncle worked for my grandfather at his grocery store. Sometimes he'd look after me when my grand-parents were away. Back then, kids could get into the Capital Theater on Saturdays and watch the matinee for six Pepsi Cola bottle caps. Your uncle used to take me there and see that I made it home all right," Sam told him.

"We'd ride the bus and that's when I learned the world wasn't a fair place. There was a sign at the front of the bus that read 'colored to the rear.' A white line was painted on the floor and all the 'colored folks' had to sit behind it. I loved your uncle and it hurt me to see him treated less than human," Sam shook his head and snuffed his cigarette in the sand.

"I would cry when we were separated. Sometimes we were lucky and we would find two seats together on opposite sides of the line and then I felt safe.

"But that ended when we got to the theater because they wouldn't let us sit together there either. We'd buy our popcorn and Pepsi, then the usher would seat me in the main auditorium. Your uncle had to sit in the balcony with the other black people."

Kareem shifted nervously as Sam pressed his point.

"I remember one day after the movie, I asked Willie why things had to be that way. He picked me up, held me in his arms, and comforted me. It's the work of the devil, he said. He told me not to cry. He said we're all God's children. And when the roll is called up yonder, we'll all be the same color. Then I felt better."

"Well, maybe so," Kareem's posture softened somewhat. "But if you black, da opportunity don't be da same as if you white."

"Kareem, get off the poor black-boy-victim crap. Maybe it was true years ago, but today the playing field is more level. You have the same shot at life as any white man."

"Yeah. Den learn me sump'm sides nigga woik. Get me outa da ditch."

"Climb out of the ditch, Kareem. I started my career right where you are, digging ditches. It didn't take me long to figure out that the sooner I learned what was going on, the sooner I wouldn't have to be doing *nigga* work, as you say. If you want to go somewhere, the sky is the limit. I can't pull you out of the ditch, son. But if you want to climb, I'll give you a hand."

"You mean you'd learn me?"

"Yes, Kareem. If that's what you want."

Kareem stood a moment looking perplexed.

"Here's what I want you to do," Sam said, eyeing Kareem intensely. "You go home and think about it. Either you can cling to the radical shit your buddies down at the pool hall tell you, or you can face the truth. Now, either come back with a different attitude, or don't come back at all."

Kareem limped to Mister Willie's car, rubbing his back as he went along. Without a word, he got in the car, cranked the engine and drove away.

27

The following morning Sam walked into the job trailer to find Mister Willie waiting on him.

"Good morning, Mister Willie. Are you feeling better?"

"Yes suh, yes suh. Heap better. I don't know what choo said to Tyrone, but he sho be talkin' sense for a change."

"I just put it to him straight," Sam explained. If he wants to help himself, I'll help him. You know that, Mister Willie."

"Thank you suh. You a good man. Come here, boy," Mister Willie yelled toward the tool room. "Tyrone got sump'm he wanna say to you, suh."

Just then Kareem walked out of the tool room with his hat in his hand. He walked over to Sam, hesitated a moment, then made his plea.

"I sorry for da way I been doin'. I want to learn sump'm better than sellin' crack rocks. I wanna be like Mistah Oliver. I wanna woik. Learn me, Mistah Sam. Show me how to keep da bubble tween da lines."

"All right, Kareem. I'll give you the benefit of the doubt and take you at your word. Where you go from here is up to you. Now show me what you can do."

The gratification Sam felt at that moment was worth the irritation Kareem had caused. Sam hoped Kareem's word was as good as his intentions seemed to be. Time would tell.

The work week went well. By Wednesday afternoon, Kareem had mastered "ditch grading 101." Sam was pleasantly surprised. Kareem's disposition had made a 180 degree turn. Thursday, Sam hired another laborer to help Mister Willie with the ditches and to replace Kareem. Sam charged Jerry with the responsibility of teaching Kareem how to operate the melting pot, and by Friday morning, Kareem was putting pipe together and bringing melted lead for the plumbers to make their joints. He also replaced his Malcolm X hat with one advertising Sandpiper Plumbing Supply Company.

28

At five-thirty that afternoon, Brit found Sam sitting at the drawing table in the job trailer. She was excited because the management at the Shipwreck had agreed to let her have Sunday off. Her father had bought her a brand new under-water camera and Brit wanted to go diving. It had been weeks since she'd been, and she was glad Wilton wanted to go as well.

"Isn't this wonderful," Brit said, removing the camera from the box and placing it on the blue prints in front of Sam.

"Looks complicated," Sam smiled as he held the camera and looked at the dials and switches.

"Oh Sam'o, there's nothing to it," she said, playfully slapping his arm.

"Not if you know what you're doing," said Sam. He put his arm around her waist and drew her near.

"I stopped by to give you a message," Brit said, smiling as she mussed his hair.

"What's up?"

"Tom Marshall called the lounge just after lunch and asked me to ask you to drop by his house before you come home."

"What does he want?"

"He didn't say. He just wanted you to stop by."

"All right, baby. I'll be leaving here as soon as I finish this little bit of work. I'll stop by and see what he wants." Sam kissed her good-bye and she went out the door.

When Sam arrived at the Marshall's house, he saw that a second story had been added and the primary floor space had been increased. As he walked up the drive, he saw Tom standing down at his dock. He was leaning over the rail watching the tide come in when Sam greeted him.

"Hey, Tom. What's going on?"

"Thanks for stoppin' by, Sammy."

Tom straightened up, pushed his ball cap back, and wiped his brow with his shirt sleeve. He leaned over the railing once again and looked into the water. He smiled and a placid look came over him.

"Mighty peaceful down here on my dock, ain't it? Look, see there, the tides comin' in. You see those ripples on the water down yonder at the creek bend? That's my supper. Look! Here they come now. Get me that cast net over there and step out of my way."

Sam reached down into a five-gallon bucket and handed Tom the cast net. As feeble and shaky as Tom was, his movement was meticulous and rhythmic. He put one thread of the net between his teeth, draped half the net over his forearm, and stalked his prey. With the grace of a ballet dancer he spun the net over the railing. It opened perfectly into a disk and glided through the air. The lead weights plunged into the water, pulling the net down to the creek bed and capturing all that it encompassed.

"Watch this, Sammy. You let it settle for a second or two, and you yank the draw string to gather em up, then you haul em in."

Tom slowly pulled the net's cord that was tethered to his wrist, and the net began to come out of the water. Suddenly the water boiled as the trapped fish made their futile effort to escape. He pulled until he retrieved the net and its bounty. Standing on the dock, he raised the top of the net over his head and released the draw string. Three two-pound mullet then thrashed about on the dock.

"Pick em up, Sammy, and put em in that bucket over there before they flop back into the creek. Easy as shootin' fish in a barrel, ain't it? You just gotta know what you're doin'. It's all in the wrist. Look down there. In a minute there'll be a whole mess more of em swimmin' through here. We got enough, though. Never take more than you need. They ain't fit to eat unless you kill em, and gut em, and cook em right away." He laid the cast net over the railing and dried his hands on his trousers.

"Yesiree, Sammy. It's mighty peaceful. I love livin' on this creek. When I'm down here fishin', or out in my boat, I don't let a whole lot worry me. Jan fell in love with it too the first time I brought her here. You know, the first time I ever nailed her was right here on this dock, right there where you're standin'. I met Jan at the Shipwreck late one night and it changed my life," Sam listened as Tom reminisced.

"She'd been there drinkin' since happy hour," Tom went on, "so by the time I introduced myself to her, she was easy pickins. I told her about my dock and how peaceful it is here, and she wanted to see it right away. It was a beautiful night, all the stars were shinin', and there was a nice breeze blowin' right out of the south. I was a lot stronger back then, and Jan wasn't so big as she is now, so it was no problem helpin' her down here.

"She said she had somethin' to show me, and she made me shut my eyes. When she told me to open em, I damn near fainted. Sam, she didn't have a stitch of clothes on, and you know, she was a sight to behold.

"She was even more beautiful back then than she is now, if you can believe that. She just stood there smilin' at me, then she fell down, right there where you see that broken two-by-four. That's where I put it to her that night and nothin's been the same in my life since.

"After I got done plowin' her field, I went up to the house to get us a drink and a blanket.

When I got back she'd already passed out. She was lyin' there with her mouth open and snorin' like a grizzly bear. I covered her up and laid down next to her. She felt so good, Sammy, I just knew it was gonna be the start of somethin' big. Yeah. It was somethin' big all right. C'mon. Grab that bucket of fish so I can get em cleaned."

Sam picked up the bucket and followed Tom to the cleaning table. Tom reached into an Igloo cooler for two bottles of Miller Lite. He twisted the cap off one of the bottles and handed it to Sam. Then Tom cringed with pain and grabbed his arm.

"What's wrong with your arm, Tom?"

Tom rolled up his shirt sleeve and exposed a blue lump on his forearm. It looked to be the size of a goose egg. His arm was swollen all the way up to his shoulder. The tissue around the lump had turned gray, and red streaks ran up his arm.

"I ain't lyin' about it no more. I been lyin' about it for two years now. Jan did it to me," said Tom. His eyes were wide and he stared blankly.

"Why the hell would she do something like that?" Sam shook his head.

"She said the house is 'fucked up' and it's my fault. She said she hated me and wouldn't never forgive me for it. I told her to sit her fat ass down and shut up. That's when she came at me like a whirlin' dervish. She hit me with a ball peen hammer hard as she could swing it."

"Son of a bitch, Tom. Did you call the cops?"

"No. She didn't mean to hit me as hard as she did. She told me so."

"I can't believe she'd do such a thing," Sam said, looking at the wound. "Are you saying all those accidents you've had weren't really accidents at all?"

"Yep, that's what I'm tellin' ya," Tom's false teeth rattled as he spoke. "She never said she was sorry before, though. But this time it's different. She promised me it wouldn't never happen again. And you know what, Sammy? I believe her."

Sam eyed him skeptically. "Why did you want me to come over?"

"Well, I wanted you to take a look around and tell me if everything looks okay to you. Clovis is puttin' up sheet rock tomorrow. But it don't really matter no more."

"I don't mind, Tom. I told you I'd help you if I could."

"Thanks, Sammy. You look around while I clean these fish," Tom picked up his butcher knife, and Sam went inside.

Walking through the back door, Sam noticed the vinyl siding was nailed improperly. The nails were driven in too tight for the vinyl to expand and contract with the change of temperature. Eventually the vinyl would crack and buckle.

Inside the kitchen, by the bay window, sat a wooden table and four chairs. Sam had never seen the like. He was amazed that the Marshalls were actually living in the house during major renovation.

Naturally, the first thing Sam looked at was the plumbing. The water piping was gray polybutylene with copper fittings and crimp rings. The material was sub-standard, and at the time, a class-action law suit against the manufacturer was in progress. Because of severe leakage from faulty fittings, homeowners nationwide had lost millions of dollars.

The drainage system was a fiasco. Nothing was properly vented and several drain pipes were falling backwards. Sam walked around the corner and up the stairs. When he reached the second floor, he smelled a noxious odor that he immediately recognized as sewer gas. Upon further investigation, he discovered the source. The main vent stack had not been extended through the roof, and volatile methane was pouring in through the stack. The gas had accumulated in such concentration that Sam prudently extinguished his cigarette.

The laundry room was adjacent to the upstairs bath. Sam squeezed around the sheet rock that was stacked against the stud wall in the hallway. He made his way to the laundry and there, inside the washing machine outlet box, was a green county sticker signed by Shaneeka Holmes.

"Well, I'm a son of a bitch," Sam said. "If this don't take the cake."

Next to the green sticker was a white one approving the air conditioning system. Sam climbed into the attic, looked around and drew a blank. The duct work was not yet installed. He went back downstairs thinking he might have missed something but seeing was believing. Shaneeka Holmes had approved an air conditioning system that didn't exist.

Sam didn't bother checking the wiring because he wasn't qualified to know whether it was right or not. He did look into the electrical panel box to see if the county sticker was there. It was.

Walking back toward the kitchen, Sam dreaded telling Tom what he'd learned. When he went back around the corner he caught wind of an awful odor coming from the Marshall's bedroom. The bedroom door was slightly ajar. When Sam opened it and went in, what he found nearly made him lose his lunch.

Jan was on the floor, stark naked, on her back, and lying in a pile of excrement. Her arms and legs were spread eagle, and she was fiercely clinging to a half-empty bottle of vodka. Her mouth was agape and her tongue hung from the corner of it. Her eyes were wide open and crossed. She appeared to be staring at the ball peen hammer that was buried between her eyes, deep into her skull.

Sam hurriedly turned to leave the room, and he was immediately shocked again. Tom was standing there with a deranged look on his face and his butcher knife in his hand. Sam jumped back in alarm. Tom lowered the knife, looked down at the corpse, and smiled gently.

"She was drunk as a coot when she started in on me. But look at her now, Sammy. Ain't she beautiful? In all the time I've known her, I ain't never seen her look so peaceful."

Sam tried to breathe normally as he slowly edged around Tom and toward the door. Tom's eyes were vacant. It was as if the lights were on but nobody was home.

"She'll be stinkin' up the place pretty soon if we don't get her outa here, Sammy. We gotta drag her down to the dock and throw her into the creek."

"I don't know, Tom. Maybe we ought to call somebody," Sam said, backing away.

"You think we oughta call the police?"

"Yeah, that'd probably be a good idea."

"Would you do it for me Sammy? I just don't like talkin' to em."

Tom walked back into the kitchen and went to the stove. He rolled a piece of mullet into beaten egg, dragged it through a bowl of corn meal, and placed it into a pan of hot grease. Sam went to the living room to use the telephone. He picked up the phone and dialed the number.

"Tybee Island Police Department," the voice came over the line. "This is Sergeant Braxton."

"Billy...this is Sam Lewis."

"Hey Sam. Congratulations. I'm looking forward to kissing the bride. What's up?"

"I'm at Tom Marshall's house. You'd better get somebody over here. He's killed his wife."

"Say what!?"

"I'm not kidding, Billy. I feel like I'm right in the middle of a Stephen King movie."

"Are you sure she's dead."

"Yeah, I'm sure."

"Where is Tom?"

"He's in the kitchen, frying mullet."

"Is he armed?"

"Not really," Sam said to him. " Just with a spatula."

"All right, Sam. Stay calm. Someone is on the way."

29

"Brit, please, make me a drink. Straight up. Make it a double...and hurry."

"Sam'o, what's wrong. You're white as a sheet."

Sam poured down the drink and made himself another. He fell back on the couch and Brit sat beside him. Sparing Brit the gory details, he told her about the Marshalls.

"It was the damndest thing I ever saw, Brit," Sam said, shaking his head. "The damndest thing I ever saw."

"Sounds like the old bloke's got a few roos loose in the top paddock."

"I don't know, baby. I guess Jan just hit him one time too many."

"Well that explains a lot." I couldn't imagine anyone being *that* accident prone. What did the police say?"

"They want me to go to the station tomor-row and file a report."

"Did they take him to jail?"

"No. They took him to the hospital. His arm was looking gangrenous. When he gets out of there, he's going to Georgia Regional for psy-chiatric observation."

"Do you think they'll bring charges against him?"

"I don't think so. This isn't the first time the cops have been called over there after Jan attacked him. Just last week they were called after she hit him in the head with a hair brush. It's all on record. But the poor guy never would press charges. Since they can establish a pattern of abuse, they'll probably call it self-defense."

"I hope so," said Brit. "I've always felt sorry for Tom."

"Yeah. Me too. Tom was right about one thing though."

"What's that?"

"I've never seen her look so peaceful either."

30

At 4:30 Sunday morning a decisive chill

was in the air when Brit, Sam, and Wilton, arrived at Lazaretto Creek. A disconcerting breeze was blowing from the north that threatened to ruin the days diving. It was the middle of March, so taking a dive trip was a crap shoot.

"What do you think?" Sam asked as Jerry emerged from the cabin of his Hatteras. Jerry had been up nearly an hour trying to decide what the weather was going to do.

"I don't know. Ya'll have gone to the trouble of getting up and coming down here. We might as well give it a shot."

The three loaded their food, a big cooler of ice, and their dive gear onto the boat. A certain exuberance came over everyone when the two powerful diesel engines rumbled to life.

Sam stood on the dock awaiting Jerry's signal to untie the rope in preparation to cast off. When the order came, Sam loosed the stern line and pushed the rear of the big boat away from the dock. He quickly moved to the front and unfastened the bow line. He gave the bow a shove then jumped on board.

Sam secured the line to a cleat and pulled the fender off the starboard side onto the bow. Then he made his way to the stern. Sam, Brit, and Wilton climbed the ladder and walked onto the bridge where Jerry was carefully maneuvering the boat down the creek. Jerry anxiously listened to the weather broadcast that was coming over the marine radio.

"Hmm," said Jerry. "They're calling for winds light and variable and seas less than three feet. Maybe they know something I don't. There were half-inch swells in my coffee cup earlier this morning," he said with a grin.

The boat slowly rippled the water as it moved through the no-wake zone heading toward open ocean, and freedom to gun the throttle. When Jerry passed the last channel marker, he punched the numbers 453445:611958 into his loran, and plotted course to the Anchor Ledge, thirty-six nautical miles ahead of them. Then he punched another button and the compass heading for their destination magically appeared on the loran's digital screen.

"Steer a little north of 130 degrees," Jerry said, passing the helm to Sam.

Sam enjoyed driving the Hatteras and relying on electronic components to guide his way to an exact location in the middle of nowhere. The wind was still blowing strong, and the sea seemed angry. The ride was choppy, and Jerry feared the weather would only get worse.

Once properly at sea, the wind shifted and

blew from the south at a warm and steady pace. The ocean was calm two hours later when the Hatteras sped by the last sea buoy on the way to the Snapper Banks.

Jerry returned to his cabin and crawled back into bed. He fell asleep shortly after they passed the buoy. During the balance of the voyage to the Anchor Ledge, Sam, Brit and her father passed the time with jokes and good conversation.

Another hour went by, before the loran's alarm went off, alerting Sam that he was within a half-mile of the ledge. The alarm brought Jerry back from his sleep and Sam heard him stumbling to the bridge. He put his hand on the back of Sam's chair and scanned the loran.

"I'll take it from here, Sam," he said. "Go get the buoy ready."

The buoy was a thirty-gallon plastic drum with a 115 foot nylon line attached to it. On the other end was a five-foot chain and a boat anchor. Sam carefully wound the line around the drum all the way to the anchor chain and sat at the back of the boat awaiting word to throw the buoy.

The boat moved slowly while Jerry observed the color screen on his depth finder. The digits varied as the sonar sounded the bottom and the signal returned: 99 feet, 98, 97, 99, 96...108.

"Drop it!" Jerry yelled.

Sam threw the buoy over the stern, and it spun wildly as the anchor reeled off the cord and plunged toward the bottom. When it came to a stop, Jerry circled the buoy and observed the colored images on the depth finder representing thousands of fish, all different sizes, swimming at depths ranging from sixty-five to 110 feet.

The divers would go into the water in teams of two. Each team would make two dives that day. There would be a four-hour surface interval after their first dive before they could safely go back into the water. Brit wanted to dive with her father.

Wilton and Brit made preparations to take the plunge. Sam helped Brit pull on her wet suit, then helped her with the heavy steel tank. Brit and Wilton squeezed a little tooth paste into their masks, smeared it over their lenses, then rinsed them out in the water. The paste served as a de-fogging agent. Commercial preparations were available but tooth paste worked better and it was cheaper.

Brit and Wilton stepped over the transom and on to the swim platform. Sam handed Brit her camera, and she adjusted her face mask. He gave her a kiss and she placed the regulator between her teeth.

"Be careful, baby, and stay together," Sam cautioned her.

"Here, Wilton, take this with you." Sam gave Wilton his spear gun and his rubber bullet holder filled with bullets.

"I don't plan on doing any hunting, mate. But taking it is a good idea. You never know what's down there that may want to make a meal of us."

Jerry brought the boat back around to the buoy. He throttled down and put the gear in neutral. When directly by the buoy, Brit and her father held their masks firmly and stepped in. Sam watched them swim down the anchor line until they disappeared.

All along the Georgia coast, rock ledges ran at depths starting at eighty feet and dotted the ocean floor, all the way to the Gulf Stream. That area was the fishing grounds known as the "Snapper Banks." The mouth of some ledges, from the top of the rock to the sandy bottom, was more than twelve feet. The ledges narrowed like wedges until the rock met the ocean floor.

Many species of tropical fish inhabited the

ledges, as well as several varieties of food fish. Giant spiny lobsters, moray eels and sea cucumbers lived there as well. Nurse sharks and sea rays hid in the crevices. Bull and sand tiger sharks patrolled the sand. Brit would have no shortage of subjects to photograph with her new Nikon.

The boat circled the buoy and Sam watched for air bubbles for the twenty minutes Brit and her father were down. After eighteen minutes down time, Sam climbed the tuna tower to look for them when they surfaced. After a few minutes Sam saw his spear gun sticking out of the water fifty yards south of the buoy. He looked through his field glasses and saw Brit bobbing beside Wilton. She held her arms over her head in a circle that was a sign letting Sam and Jerry know they were okay. Jerry gunned the engines and they headed to pick up the divers.

The boat slowed as it pulled up alongside Brit and Wilton. They climbed onto the swim platform, and handed Sam the camera and gun.

"How was it?" Sam asked

"Wonderful," said Brit. "There are a lot of big fish down there."

"Did you get any good pictures?"

"Oh yes. I used a whole roll of film!"

Brit and her father came back aboard then Sam and Jerry suited up. Wilton took the helm and brought the boat back around in the direction of the buoy.

"We're gonna tear em up today, Sam," Jerry said as they traveled toward it.

Sam checked his bullets. He'd painted the primers with fingernail polish to keep water out. He'd also painted around the area where the lead met the casings. He was apprehensive as always before a day's first dive at the banks. He strapped on his weight belt, donned his tank, and slipped into his flippers.

Sam sat on the port side of the boat and kissed Brit good-bye. He slid on his mask, put the regulator in his mouth, and waited for Wilton to reach the buoy. Jerry was sitting on the starboard rail giving Sam thumbs up when Wilton yelled they were beside the buoy. With spear guns in one hand, securing their face masks and regulators with the other, they fell over backwards and bailed into the water.

The ocean was cold, sixty-three degrees, but because of all the other stimuli, they never felt it. As soon as Sam got his bearings he swam toward the anchor line and started his descent. He turned the knob on the stock of his spear gun to the safe position and prepared to load.

By then he had descended seven feet and felt pressure on his ears. He held his nose and blew, equalizing the pressure, then loaded a cartridge into the power-head. He equalized again and pulled back the first elastic band on his gun. He equalized a third time then pulled back the second band. Now ready for the hunt, he relaxed and enjoyed his descent, equalizing every six feet or so.

Sam's apprehension left him and was replaced by an eerie calm and sense of well-being when he saw the bottom gradually come into focus. The narcotic effect of nitrogen under pressure had lulled him into his feeling of serenity. It was a mixed blessing. His thought process was slightly slowed but that gave him time to think things out; he wouldn't panic if something went wrong.

Sam effortlessly floated downward until his knees hit the bottom, stirring up a cloud of sand. He looked up and saw Jerry ten feet above swimming toward the ledge. The visibility was good, forty feet or more. Sam remembered days when the visibility was sixty feet at the Banks, but other times he had literally bumped into the bottom before he saw it.

He pushed the inflater button and injected just enough air into his vest to make him neu-

trally buoyant, then followed Jerry to the ledge.
When Jerry reached the ledge he spotted a
school of large grouper twenty feet to the south.
Sam watched as Jerry approached the fish.
Then Sam swam away from him in a northerly
direction.

The ghostly sea-scape, was as always,
mysteriously quiet. The only audible sound was
Sam's own breathing as he drew air off the regulator and the rumbling noise of the bubbles billowing around his head when he exhaled. He
continued swimming north, shining his light
under the ledge, and alternately looking straight
ahead. The unearthly silence shattered when
the loud, vibrating, *thonk* of Jerry's exploding
power-head startled him from his dreamlike
exploration.

"Shit," Sam shouted into his mouth piece.
"Scares me every time. You're one up on me
eh." Sam had a habit of talking to himself
through his regulator and his voice sounded
garbled when it permeated into the water.

He continued up the ledge seeing nothing
worth shooting. He'd seen a few grouper in the
five-to-ten pound range but was holding out for
the big one. He was swimming by a large Log-
gerhead turtle when he heard it again. *Thonk.*

"Damn, Jerry," he muttered. "Gonna

skunk me again, ain't you."

Just then, the outline of a large silver fish resembling a giant carp, was mystically taking form through the blue haze. Sam's adrenaline soared and his heart thudded as he slowly approached the fish. That was no carp. The light red color of the fish appeared silver green at that depth. Sam turned off the safety and held his breath while drawing a bead on his prey. The huge red snapper was looking right at him as he closed in. Slowly the fish turned broadside and Sam pulled the trigger. *Thonk.*

The three-fifty-seven hit it right behind and just above his eye, a kill shot. The fish turned upside down and quivered a moment while a green cloud of blood streamed from its head.

Sam reached for his stringer while swimming for his fish. The stringer looked like a big safety pin and could hold four or five such fish. He shoved the pointed end into the fish's eye, through its head and out through the other eye. He clipped it shut then unwound the fifteen feet of string that was secured to the stringer. Sam always kept his dead fish at a distance in case a shark or barracuda spotted them and took a bite out of Sam instead of the fish.

Having captured his supper, he looked at

his bottom timer and saw he'd been down nineteen minutes. He kicked off the bottom and started his ascent, fish trailing below. The water temperature warmed appreciably as Sam neared the surface. At ten feet he leveled off and maintained his depth three minutes for an unrequired safety decompression stop. Then he continued his ascent until his head broke through the surface.

Sam raised his gun high in the air to make himself visible as possible. The boat was in view and after a few moments, Brit spotted him. The engines roared, the boat lurched forward, and Wilton was on his way.

Wilton cut the engines back to idle speed twenty yards before the Hatteras glided to a stand-still, fifteen feet from where Sam surfaced. Sam kicked to the boat's hull. Brit beamed when she took his spear gun from him. Jerry was already on board. Sam handed him the lanyard and he gathered the line, hoisting the trophy-sized red snapper onto the deck.

Sam slid out of his buoyancy control vest, housing his tank and regulator, and floated it toward Jerry. Jerry grabbed the ensemble by the carry-handle and dragged it on board. Sam pulled himself onto the swim platform, then stood up; slapping little waves licked his calves.

Brit removed his mask and laughed over the ghost of the mask's red outline embossed on his face. Sam stepped over the transom, dripping wet, and removed his flippers.

"What did you get?" he asked, looking at the red ring Jerry's mask had left behind.

"A couple of grouper," Jerry answered, tossing his head toward his kill.

Lying on the deck were two grouper that looked to weigh twenty-five pounds each. Laying beside them was Sam's fish.

"Grab the scales out of my tackle box, please, Brittany," Jerry said. "I wanna see how much that big one weighs."

Jerry hooked the scales into the fish and raised it from the deck.

"Thirty-eight pounds," Jerry said after he dropped the snapper back down.

"Pick it up, Sam'o and stand back by the stern. I want to get a shot of you and your fish," said Brit. Sam held up the fish while Brit took the picture then he dropped the fish into the cooler.

During the next four hours, while the excess nitrogen infused into their bodies by four atmospheres of pressure was being metabolized, there was plenty of time to go fishing. Everyone baited their hooks and dropped their rigs near to the bottom. The action was fast as it usually was at the Snapper Banks.

While they fished, they discussed the dive and considered where they might go for their second one. Wilton caught a small vermilion snapper. He lifted it out of the water for a moment then let it sink back to the bottom. After a few minutes, his pole bent over and the reel sang as something quickly stripped away the line. Wilton held the pole fast and braced himself against the transom. After three hundred feet of line was reeled away, the fish turned and Wilton began reeling it in.

"I hope it's not the pretty mermaid I met while I was down there," he said, fighting to gain some line.

"Maybe it's her ugly sister," said Jerry. "I met *her* out here once. She was a freak of nature. Her top half was a fish and her bottom half was a girl."

"Did you have a plastic bag to put over her head," laughed Wilton.

"Oh, daddy, that's disgusting," Brit complained.

Twenty minutes passed and the fish was still going strong 100 feet from the boat. In another twenty minutes the fish was beginning to tire, as was Wilton. Finally it was within sight.

It was a wahoo! And it was a big one. The fish made one last run then seemed to give up and accept its fate.

Wilton reeled it alongside the boat, and Jerry gaffed it just behind its head. Together Jerry and Wilton hoisted the long slender fish onto the boat. Brit gave them the scales and they weighed it. Seventy-two pounds!

"Hey Wilton," said Sam. "I'll trade you that snapper for it. Wahoo is the best eating fish I know."

"Not a chance, mate. I'll cut away the strong red meat, and it'll be better than chicken. No, no Sam'o. This one is bound for Brisbane."

"Well shibber me timbers and blow me down," said Sam. "How about trading a steak for a steak?"

"Only if you invite me over and cook it up for us," Wilton smiled.

The surface interval time passed quickly. Most of the fish caught were black sea bass weighing one to two pounds. Brit caught an eighteen-pound grouper, a ten-pound red snapper, a couple of nice-sized trigger fish, and many black bass. Jerry and Wilton did well that day too. Sam didn't fish much; he was having too much fun watching Brit.

When time came for the second dive, ev-

eryone was getting tired and ready to get a move
on. They reeled in their lines and Jerry maneu-
vered the boat beside the buoy. As Sam pulled
in the buoy line, Brit wound it around the buoy.
Shortly thereafter, the boat was planed up and
running toward the next dive site.

Brit and Wilton got back into their wet
suits, donned their gear and bailed overboard.
While they were down, Sam and Jerry discussed
the work that had to be done the following day.
Jerry was pleased at the progress Kareem had
been making.

"He's a lot smarter than he acts sometimes," Jerry said. "And he's starting to back
off from all that shuckin' and jivin' too."

"Yeah," Sam nodded. "A lot of that was
just a put on. Maybe he'll make a good plumber
one day."

"If he doesn't it sure won't be your fault."
Jerry checked his watch to see how long it was
before Brit and Wilton were to surface.

"It'll just take some time, that's all." Sam
lit a cigarette."

"You're a patient man," laughed Jerry. "I
would have put an end to him the first day on
the job. Say, speaking of putting an end to
things, what about old Tom Marshall. He sure
took care of his number one problem. I'll bet

she was rank, lying there stiff as a board," Jerry
wrinkled his nose and turned down his mouth.

"Not a pretty sight," Sam rolled his eyes.
"But I don't know what to do about problem
number two. I'll give you two guesses who
signed off on the inspection stickers. Make that
three guesses and the first two don't count."

"Sweet Shaneeka, huh? I don't know that
much about the business but it sure looks like
someone should be inspecting the inspectors."

"Maybe. I don't know," Sam said, watching Brit's and Wilton's bubbles. "But something
has to be done. I was going to call the Secre-
tary of State but Clyde threatened me with un-
employment if I make any more waves."

"What's it going to take to make people
wake up?" Jerry asked.

"I don't know, Jerry. I really don't know."

Sam was more relaxed his second dive,
making his way down the buoy line. Five minutes into the dive he spotted something he'd
rarely seen that time of year. A spiny lobster,
that looked to weigh twelve pounds or better,
was laying motionless on the ocean floor beside
a clump of sponges. The unusually warm
weather prompted the large crustacean to crawl
in from the Gulf Stream weeks before the nor-
mal migration time. Sam hovered a few feet

above it and aimed his gun. *Thonk.* When the dust settled, he threaded his stringer through the hole in the lobster's empty head. This big ole bug will feed Brit and me a couple of times, and we'll still have plenty left for lobster stew, he thought.

31

Brit stood on the port side of the Hatteras watching one set of air bubbles that hadn't moved from the vicinity of the buoy. She worried because she new Sam and Jerry were separated. Wilton circled the buoy in an increasingly wide circumference in an effort to locate the second set of bubbles. The divers had been down seven minutes when a thick cloud of smoke belched from the vessel's exhaust pipes and both engines choked down.

Wilton tried, in vain, several attempts to re-start the engines while the boat drifted away with the current. The loran was adjusted to display the vessel's relative position and the numbers steadily changed as they drifted. Brit watched the buoy grow smaller while the boat moved farther and farther away. Wilton spoke into the marine radio and broadcast the international distress call.

"Mayday, Mayday, our position is 453182
: 611736. We have divers down and we are dis-
abled and drifting. Repeat. Mayday, Mayday..."

32

Perched on his knees beside the anchor
at the bottom of the buoy line, Jerry slapped
his emergency second-stage regulator in an attempt to make it stop free-flowing precious air
into the water. He was nine minutes into the
fifteen-minute dive and his air pressure was
already down to a thousand pounds. He'd just
picked the damned thing up from the repair
shop and was none too happy about it. Finally,
realizing the futility of his efforts, he ascended,
cursing all the while.

When he broke through the surface, the
buoy was bobbing about in the water like an
angler's float but the boat was nowhere in sight.
He filled his vest full of air and floated as high
as possible, affording him the best view. When
he crested the top of a two-foot wave, he saw
the boat a hundred yards to the north. He
reached behind his head and shut off the valve
to stop the free flow of air through his second
stage, stuffed his snorkel in his mouth, and
began swimming.

33

Sam swam along the ledge hoping to find more lobster but he didn't see any. A twenty-pound grouper then hung dead beside the lobster on his stringer. He was fourteen minutes into the dive when, out from the corner of his eye, he spotted a large bull shark cruising his catch, fifteen feet behind him. He spun around and quickly pulled the stringer back to himself, aimed his gun and waited for the shark to get close enough for a good shot. The shark began to circle, darting in and out as it moved.

Suddenly, Sam spotted two more the same size swimming erratically, alerting him that he and his catch were about to be the object of a feeding frenzy. He removed the fish from the stringer, dropped it to the bottom, hit the inflator button and rocketed toward the surface. Looking down, as he streaked upward, he watched the sharks ravage his grouper.

At sixty feet he dumped most of the air from his vest, slowing his ascent. At fifty feet, he stopped dead in the water then began to descend, swimming in a southerly direction. At seventy-five feet, the dark outline of the ledge was clearly visible. After following the ledge a few minutes, the buoy line came into view.

When he'd launched himself off the bottom, he had been down sixteen minutes, over-staying his no-decompression time limit by one minute. He had traveled nearly sixty feet upward in ten seconds when safety dictated a proper ascension rate of no less than sixty seconds for that distance. Thankful he'd found the buoy line, he climbed it at five seconds per foot until he reached forty feet, then dropped the lobster to the end of the lanyard. He hung there and watched the "bug" dangle safely below him.

He knew he was courting a severe case of decompression sickness: the bends. If he'd gone directly to the surface after his latest escapade, the nitrogen that flowed in solution through his veins, would return to a gaseous state. The gas would boil in his blood like carbonic acid in a bottle of soda-pop opened too soon after being dropped. At best, the nitrogen would lodge in his joints, causing excruciating pain and a costly trip to the decompression chamber. At worst, well... he didn't want to think about it.

Looking at his plastic, water-proof decompression tables, he calculated his decompression time. The tables made no provision for emergency ascent so he tripled the time indicated. Jerry always pumped the air tanks to the maximum rated pressure and Sam's air consumption was good despite the run-in with the sharks. He still had eighteen hundred pounds of air.

He hung at forty feet and worried about Brit. He knew she was thinking the worst. After seven minutes he went to thirty feet and hung another seven minutes then he went to twenty to hang for ten.

Abruptly, it occurred to him that he hadn't heard the boat engines running. In fact, the boat should have been right on top of him and he should have been seeing Brit's face through the surface, looking down at his bubbles. She should have swam down and checked on him and taken his catch back aboard the boat for safety's sake. That's the way it always worked when someone stayed too long and had to decompress. The dark hull of the boat looming above had always been comforting while he hung there by himself. Something was wrong. Something was very wrong. Sam never felt so alone.

The next twenty minutes were the longest ones of his life. He wanted to surface but he dared not. He forced himself to follow proper procedure. He ascended to ten feet and stayed another ten minutes, then for the first time in what felt like ages, he saw the light of day.

34

"What happened, Wilton?" Jerry demanded, urgently lifting his leg over the transom. "Quick, help me out of my gear."

"The engines just died. They wouldn't restart so I sent out a Mayday and gave the position close to the buoy."

"Is somebody on the way?" Jerry asked.

"Yeah, three boats radioed they were close by and they're heading this way now."

"Hand me my tool box," Jerry said, unhinging the hatch cover.

Brit watched Jerry work on the engines as the minutes ticked away.

35

Above Sam was empty blue sky; around him was a vast watery desert. He slowly turned completely around in hopes of seeing a boat but nothing was in sight. His only comforts were the buoy, his gun, and the nine remaining three-fifty-seven cartridges.

He was exceedingly fortunate and he knew it. If he hadn't found the buoy, he would have been helplessly adrift. If he'd lacked the knowledge, self-control, or air to properly decompress, he would have been very sick by then. Maybe dying. The wind and water was calm; that was in his favor. Heavy seas would hamper the search, if there was one, and quickly sap his strength.

Thoughts of making provisions for survival raced through his head. He made sure his light was off to conserve the batteries, in the event he wasn't to be rescued by nightfall. He turned off his air supply and breathed through his snorkel while scanning the water below for any unwelcome marine activity. What if the wind picked up and the waves increased to four or five feet?

What if it *really* got rough? He couldn't hold on to the buoy line with the ocean tossing, dragging him and the buoy with every swell. He'd cut the line and tie himself to the buoy if it came to that...that's what he'd do. He raised his face out of the water and scanned the surface. He thought he heard the grinding sound of a boat's engine when his head was in the water but nothing was visible. Sam maintained his composure. His advanced and rescue dive training was explicit about such situations. If you panic...you die. He was unshaken by the approaching dark clouds, far to the west, optimistic that help would soon arrive.

36

"I see something at three o'clock, about 150 yards," shouted the first mate of the impressive forty-foot Morgan fishing boat. She was standing on the tuna-tower, high above the deck of the lumbering vessel.

"Bring her around ninety degrees," she yelled, pointing toward the floating white object. Twenty-five feet above the ocean, she could see for miles.

The boat closed on the buoy; Sam was convinced of it now. He'd heard diesel engines! He looked behind him, and sure enough, relief was on the way. He waved his spear-gun high in the air and screamed at the top of his lungs. He knew no one could hear him, but his enthusiasm was consoling nonetheless. When the vessel was within 100 feet, he saw *Miss Judy Too*, indelibly painted on the bow.

The vessel was a popular charter fishing boat named after its skipper, Captain Judy Helmey. Captain Judy had been in radio contact with Brit since they first spotted something in the water. "We've got him in sight, Brittany, and he looks okay," relayed the captain. "We'll have him on board in a couple of minutes."

"Ripper! Thank God he's all right. Jerry

has been working frantically to get his engines started. He says to tell you he's almost done and we'll rendezvous with you shortly."

37

Sam swam toward the boat, unloading the three-fifty-seven cartridge from his power-head as a safety precaution, before handing Captain Judy the spear-gun. It was always prudent to unload before boarding a boat after a dive. An unexpected wave might have caused a slip of the foot and could have been deadly if the charge jabbed someone, or catastrophic, if it penetrated a fuel tank.

Sam pulled himself onto the swim platform and came to his feet. He removed his mask and saw four women staring at him from the other side of the transom. He pulled up his lobster and dropped it on the deck as he stepped on board.

"Who spotted me? I want to give her a big ole kiss."

"I did," chimed the first mate. "But how bout giving me that *big ole* lobster instead."

"You got it, You don't know how glad I am to see you ladies. You wouldn't believe the thoughts that went through my head the last couple of hours. What happened to Jerry's boat?"

Judy explained and it wasn't long before Jerry sped up alongside the Morgan. They transferred Sam's gear over, pulled the buoy, and were at once homeward bound. Brit fussed over Sam like a mother who'd just found her missing child, then her demeanor changed.

"You bloomin' ass," she scolded, backing away. What do you mean frightening me that way? You promised you'd stay with Jerry but instead, you were off on a wander, having a Captain Cook. You didn't give me a fair crack of the whip, Sam Lewis. And I'm mad as a cut snake."

Sam took his medicine in silence, feeling deserving of her vibrant, Aussie-style reprimand. But by the time the Hatteras raced past the first sea-buoy, all was forgiven, and the conversation had turned to cleaning fish and making supper.

38

Monday evening at Happy Hour, Wilton Hayes was sitting at the northeast corner of the bar at the Shipwreck Lounge. The wedding was less than two weeks away, and Wilton had established that corner of the bar as wedding-plan command central. As far as he was concerned, Brit was to be married for the first time and he meant to do it up right and spare no expense.

There were no such trivialities as sending out invitations. There was no need for them. Everyone was invited. Wilton rented every room at the DeSoto Beach Motel for the entire weekend of the ceremony. He worked out an arrangement with the motel manager to re-schedule all reservations previously booked the weekend of March thirty-first to a free weekend of the vacationer's choice, again, at Wilton's expense.

Earlier that day, he'd advanced Charlie Sherrill and Hat Man a thousand dollars to play for eight hours after the two o'clock Saturday afternoon ceremony. There would be another thousand coming to them after the wedding party.

There would be an open bar and no one would go away hungry or wanting a drink. Wilton had planned a celebration such as never had been seen at the DeSoto Beach Motel, and talk of the happening had spread like wild-fire throughout the little island and beyond.

39

Saturday morning, a week before the wedding, Sam finished his shower and dressed. An

hour before, he'd spoken with Wilton on the telephone and invited him over for a Bloody Mary.
Sam was excited about showing him the hand-
made, golden locket he'd bought for Brit's wedding gift. When the knock came, Sam answered
the door with a smile.

"Hey, Wilton, come on in."

"Top of the morning, mate. Lovely weather
today. Thanks for the invitation. I've been dying for one of your dandy Bloody Marys."

Wilton went to the couch and Sam went
into the kitchen. He made two spicy cocktails
with tomato juice, horseradish, Worcestershire,
Tobasco, and a little Vegemite Wilton had
brought Brit from Australia. He carried the
drinks into the living room and set them on the
coffee table beside Wilton.

"Wait till you see it. I hope I've done the
right thing; I hope she'll like it."

Sam went to the bedroom, came back with
the locket, and handed it to Wilton.

"It's beautiful," Wilton said, rubbing his
thumb over it.

The locket was pure gold with a single,
grass-green crysoberyl on the face of it. When
Wilton turned the locket a certain way, the light
caught the gem, and it shone a columbine-red
glow. Inscribed below the gem were the words,

God Is Love.

"That's an unusual stone," Wilton said. "I've never seen anything quite like it."

"It's an alexandrite, more precious than a diamond. It was mined in Russia. Open it up."

Wilton opened the locket and a wave of emotion swept over him. Tears filled his eyes as he gazed at the image he'd carried in his heart for so long. It was a picture of Gloria, Wilton's wife.

"God, she was beautiful," said Wilton with a tremble in his voice. "I loved her so." Wilton put his face in his hand and dried his eyes.

"Yes, Wilton," Sam said, wiping his own eyes, "she was beautiful. Brit looks just like her, only Gloria's eyes were blue."

"This is very thoughtful. I don't know of anything you could have gotten Brittany that would mean so much to her."

"Good. You know that's the only picture Brit has of her mother. She keeps it in her jewelry box. Sneaking it out and having it copied was no small accomplishment."

"No," said Wilton. "It wasn't. Sam'o," Wilton said with a serious tone. "I'd like to talk with you about some things. Let's take a walk down the beach."

"Sure," said Sam. "I'd like that."

Later, while walking the sands by the water, Wilton told Sam things he'd never said to anyone, save Brit.

"I was very busy with my work about the time of our wedding. I was dedicated and had little time for courtship. But I wanted our wedding night to be very special for Gloria. I couldn't take a holiday for a honeymoon because of the demands of my job," Wilton explained.

"I was searching for a unique place to take Gloria. Just before the ceremony, it came to me. She was always fond of lighthouses. I was fortunate to know the lighthouse keeper at Cape Moreton up in the Great Sandy Region. He made arrangements to get the key to the lighthouse the day of our wedding," Wilton bent over and picked up a conch shell. He examined it while they walked.

"It was a splendid honeymoon. I kept it a surprise until the very night. I shall never forget the look on Gloria's face and the sparkle in her eyes when we arrived at the cape and I showed her the key.

"She was wonderfully delighted after we climbed the tower and she discovered the preparations I'd made for us," Wilton smiled at the memory.

"In the room underneath the light chamber was a table with a whale oil lamp, two bottles of fine champagne, and a silver tray holding a bed of ice that contained two dozen mammoth prawns I'd flown in from Sydney." Wilton noticed a hermit crab inside the shell playing hide-and-seek with him.

"On the floor was a goose-down mattress, two like pillows, and a blanket. Beside our bed, was a Victrola and a stack of Gloria's favorite records," Wilton continued and handed the shell to Sam.

"It was enchanting. We made love there that night for the very first time. I didn't understand, but somehow I felt it. I knew in my heart, that Gloria had conceived. It wasn't long before we learned she was indeed with child."

Sam and Wilton continued walking the beach toward the mouth of the river. Sam listened as Wilton told the tragedy that followed.

"The next three months went well but then the trouble began. Gloria became sick, and as her pregnancy progressed, so did her sickness. By mid-term, she was deathly ill.

"The physician saw only one option to save Gloria's life. Her only hope was to terminate the life of the child. Being a Christian woman, that was out of the question." Sam pondered the ramifications had Gloria chosen to save herself.

"From then on, until Brit was born, Gloria suffered terribly." Wilton stared blankly, lost in the memory.

"I cannot describe the pain and the sadness I felt as I watched the woman I loved wither away to nothing but a shadow of what she'd once been.

"After Brit was born, Gloria struggled and prayed to hang on until she could know the child was all right. When she heard Brittany cry, she smiled that soft, wonderful smile and I kissed her cheek. Then Sam'o...she died in my arms."

They continued their walk in silence. The only sounds were crying gulls and gentle waves touching the shore. Wilton stopped a moment.

"You're very busy with your work, aren't you, Sam'o?"

"Yeah. Keeping on schedule is always a struggle."

"Brit told me you were troubled because you can't take her on holiday after the wedding."

"Yeah. I'm like you. I want our wedding night to be very special for her."

Wilton smiled as he gazed up at the Tybee lighthouse. In an instant Sam knew his mind and smiled back.

"Leave it to me, Sam'o. And don't breathe a word of it. Let it be our little secret."

40

The next few days flew by and before the couple knew it, the eve of their wedding day was upon them. Brit had asked Gloria to be her matron of honor and Gloria had graciously accepted. Brit, Sam, Gloria, Hat Man, Wilton, Jerry, and Pastor Edwin Hill, who was to officiate at the ceremony, gathered on the DeSoto property for the rehearsal. When the rehearsal was finished, everyone but Brit and Wilton went their separate ways.

Wilton and Brit stayed in the cabana that night, in keeping with tradition that the groom not see the bride before the ceremony on the day of their wedding. They spent the balance of the evening sharing their love and the joy that Brit had found happiness. They laughed, they cried, they held each other, then laughed and cried some more.

"You're both more fortunate than you probably know, Brittany," Wilton said to her before retiring for the evening. "I've seen the way you look at each other and it makes my heart soar. God bless you, my child...God bless you both."

Morning came and confusion erupted. There was much to do and little time. Wilton was a stickler for detail. He'd planned everything right down to who would occupy the thirty folding chairs facing the orchid-laden altar that was constructed down by the ocean.

The marquis under the DeSoto Beach Motel sign proclaimed "Wedding Day, Brittany and Sam. 2 p.m. You're Invited. Free Food, Drink, and Entertainment." Chefs, John and Espy, worked hard lining seven mess hall tables with their culinary best. In addition to the Shipwreck Lounge, the outside tiki bar was opened to accommodate the crowd gathering to celebrate the wedding.

In the cabana, Gloria was busy helping Brit with last-minute adjustments of her clothing and make up. Earlier that morning she'd been to Dawn's Hair Salon. Brit's hair was piled high and Dawn had laced the silky strands with baby's breath.

It was a warm, sunny day, not a cloud in the sky. Wilton, Jerry, and Hat Man stood next to Sam outside the Shipwreck, and watched him nervously pace back and forth, alternately looking at his watch and at the cabana. The four were dressed in tuxedos tailored by Elmer

Cobbs, an up-scale haberdasher from New York City. Wilton had sent his leased pilot and the Gulfstream jet to New York to bring Elmer to Savannah to take everyone's measurements and again for the final fittings.

In Sam's left coat pocket was a simple gold band with the inscription, God Is Love, engraved inside. He'd soon hand it to his best man. In his right pocket was the locket and the key to the Tybee Lighthouse Wilton had given him. Tension mounted as the final seconds ticked away. Pastor Hill had just arrived, giving everyone one less thing to fret about.

Between the Shipwreck and the cabana was a covered band stand where Hat Man and Charlie had set up their equipment. Behind the stand a heavy purple curtain stretched from the corner of the cabana to the Shipwreck. The massive curtain was fifty-feet long and isolated the wedding party from the parking lot.

Precisely at three minutes of two, Charlie placed his saxophone's mouthpiece to his lips and began the overture, an original tune called "Island Jam."

"It's time, Wilton," Sam said.

"Yes, son, it is indeed time." Wilton walked across the promenade, past the floral altar, and into the cabana. Pastor Hill made his way to

the alter and Sam handed Hat Man the ring.
Jerry looked through his rose-colored glasses
and reminded Sam. "Always make her proud,
my friend, always make her proud."

A hush fell over the crowd as Sam, Hat
Man, and Jerry walked together and took their
places in front of the Pastor. Pastor Hill nodded
at Charlie and, momentarily, Charlie stopped
blowing his horn. He pressed a button on his
computer and immediately the familiar "Wedding March" filled the spring air. Every eye was
on the cabana as Brit emerged holding her
father's arm.

"She looks like an angel," Sam said to Hat
Man. "Ain't she something."

"Yeah, Sam. God, she is beautiful."

Brit wore a summer-sky blue dress and
matching high heels with white stockings and a
white bouquet of flowers held near her heart.
Step by step, in time with the music, she and
her father walked toward the altar with Gloria
close behind. When they reached the altar, everyone faced the Pastor, the music stopped and
again there was silence.

"Dearly beloved." Pastor Hill's voice was
clear and sincere. "We are gathered here today,
in the sight of God and the presence of these
witnesses, to join Samuel Quincey Lewis and

Brittany Veronica Hayes in Holy matrimony.

"The institution of marriage is ordained by God. It is, therefore, not to be entered into lightly or unadvisedly, but reverently, soberly and in the fear of God."

Pastor Hill then said to Brit and Sam, "Here me now, as I charge you both. Your future happiness is to be found in mutual consideration, patience, kindness, confidence and affection. Do not expect perfection from one another; perfection belongs solely to God. Always be slow to anger and swift to praise and magnify each other's points of comeliness and strength and see each other through compassionate eyes. May you never take each other's love for granted, but always experience that wonder that exclaims," the pastor smiled knowingly, "out of all the world you have chosen me."

The Pastor then looked at Sam and charged him directly. "It is your duty, Sam, to be to Brittany a considerate, tender, faithful, loving husband, to counsel, comfort and cherish her in prosperity and trouble, to thoughtfully and carefully enlarge the place she holds in your life, to shelter her from danger and cherish her with unalterable affection. She has given you one of the most sacred things under Heaven, a woman's life and a woman's love. You

may bring her great joy or cause her deep sorrow. It is not what you bring her in a material
way that will make her truly happy; riches without love are nothing. The gift without the giver
is bare."

He then turned to Brit. "It is your duty,
Brittany, to be a considerate, tender, faithful
loving wife, to counsel, comfort and cherish him
in times of prosperity and trouble, to thoughtfully and carefully enlarge the place he holds in
your life, to shelter him from danger and cherish him with unalterable affection. On your life,
your love, and your devotion he will lean for
strength and inspiration. He will look to you
for encouragement, cheerfulness, and confidence. Make for him a place of refuge, a place
of love, and a place of peace.

"Please join hands and face each other."
Sam took her hands, looked into her eyes, and
basked in her radiance. The Pastor continued.

"Do you, Sam, solemnly pledge your faith
to Brittany? Do you promise to love her, comfort her, honor and keep her in sickness and in
health, forsaking all others and be devoted to
her as long as you both shall live?"

"I do."

"Do you, Brittany, solemnly pledge your
faith to Sam? Do you promise to love him, com-

fort him, honor and keep him in sickness and in health, forsaking all others and be devoted to him as long as you both shall live?"

"I do."

"Sam, do you have a token of your affection?"

"I do."

Hat Man handed the Pastor the ring. The Pastor gave the ring to Sam, told him to place it on the third finger of Brit's left hand, and to vow his pledge to her. As instructed, he placed the ring on her finger and earnestly said:

"Brittany, I promise before God to love you as I love myself, because it is written, a man shall leave his father and his mother, and shall cleave to his wife; and they shall be one flesh. For no man ever hated his own flesh, but nour-ishes and cherishes it. I promise to listen, to be kind, and to make you proud. I'll always make you proud."

When that was said, a smile came to Jerry's face and a tear fell from Wilton's eye. The Pastor again turned to Brit.

"Brittany, do you have a token of your af-fection?"

"I do."

Wilton reached into his pocket and brought out a matching gold ring with the same inscription on the inside. He gave the ring to the Pastor, who, in turn handed it to Brit with the same instructions he'd given Sam.

"Sam," she said, "I promise before God to love you forever. I'll never lie to, cheat on, steal from, or hurt you in any way whatever. Today, my prayers are answered; your precious heart is mine. Tomorrow, the next day and always, my prayers will be the same. I love you, Sam'o."

Pastor Hill paused for a moment, then looked toward the multitude of people witnessing the event.

"The wedding ring is the outward and visible sign of an inward and spiritual bond which unites two hearts in endless love. The circle is the emblem of eternity, the gold, the type of what is least tarnished and most enduring. It is to show how lasting and imperishable is the faith now pledged. Let the ring, a fit token of that which is unending, continue to be a symbol of the value, the purity, and the constancy of true wedded love, and the seal of the vows which you have both pledged.

"By the authority vested in me according to the ordinance of God and the laws of the State of Georgia, I now pronounce Sam and Brittany, husband and wife. What God has joined together, let no man put asunder. You may now seal your commitment with a kiss."

The kiss was short and tender. The audience went wild with whistles, cheers and toasts for the couple.

After a long photography session the crowd gathered, making ready for Brit to throw the bouquet. She turned and faced the ocean beside the floral altar, then threw the garland back high over her head, into the crowd.

Gloria caught it, screamed an enthusiastic *"Yes!,"* then looked for Hat Man who'd seen her catch the bouquet and disappeared into the crowd. He thought a lot of Gloria but marriage wasn't on his agenda.

After Sam and Brit cut the cake, the couple shared a glass of champagne and the celebration began in earnest. Charlie announced the time had come for Sam's and Brit's dance, Saxophone for Baby. The couple swayed to the music while the audience looked on and shared their joy.

After the song, Hat Man joined Charlie and they played straight through until the church bells down the street rang out six o'clock. Then the duo took a break to have something to eat. After a half-hour they resumed their entertaining. It was nearly nine o'clock before Brit and Sam found a moment alone.

The crowd broke into tumultuous applause appreciating Hat Man's and Charlie's entertainment. As the din subsided, Wilton made his way through the crowd to the bandstand. After Wilton whispered in Hat Man's ear, Hat Man held up his hand to quiet the crowd.

"Folks, please, give me your attention," Hat Man said to the masses.

After several pleas, the crowd quieted to a murmur. Hat Man spoke into the microphone.

"Charlie and I are gonna take an early break, but we'll be back in a few. In the meantime, Mister Hayes has something he wants to say."

Another round of applause came from the crowd as Wilton took the stand. Randy and Charlie moved away and Wilton addressed the microphone. Brit held Sam's hand and gave it a squeeze."

"I wonder what in the world he's about now, Sam'o."

"I don't know," Sam laughed. "And knowing your father, I wouldn't dare speculate," they listened as Wilton gave his oratory.

"Next to the day I married my wife, Gloria, this is unequivocally the happiest day of my life," Wilton's eyes found Brit's.

"As I see my daughter standing there in

her wedding gown, I am fondly reminded of her dear mother. Gloria died giving life to our little Brittany . . . and there was a terrible . . . unfathomable emptiness I feared I could not endure," Wilton, overcome by emotion, took a deep breath and tried to keep his voice from breaking.

"But when the small, gentle hand of this woman-child rested in mine, and I looked into those innocent, trusting little eyes, I saw her mother there, and I was comforted." Wilton locked his eyes directly on Sam's.

"Sam'o, it was no small gesture passing that same hand to you this day. But I know in my heart that Gloria smiled down at the passing. It is with absolute certainty that I say to you now, I know you will do her proud."

Sam smiled. He had to. At that moment, only a smile could stop the tears. He nodded his appreciation and concurrence.

Wilton turned his attention back to the crowd.

"I would like to thank each and every one of you for the kindness you have shown my little girl. You have all been a friend to her," Wilton paused a moment and continued.

"Nothing would please me more than to take all of you to Oz, at this very minute, that you might have a glimpse of the world from whence Brittany hails. Unfortunately, because of our personal obligations, this is not possible. So ladies and gentlemen without further ado...it is with great pleasure that I give you...*Australia!*"

Wilton nodded, the lights went dim, then the air hovered with the low, vibrating sound of a lone didgeridoo. From behind the curtain an Aborigine emerged blowing into the instrument as the spotlight followed his every move. Slowly, he went before the band stand and around the promenade, as the chilling sound became louder.

He wore the dress of his ancient people. Around his waist was a bright red, blue, and yellow cloth with swaying fringes. His hair was graying as was his long, full beard and thick mustache, that hung down and hid his upper lip. A traditional, Aboriginal head band decorated his forehead and two yellow feathers hung from it, draping onto his shoulders.

His face was painted with white dots that circled his eyes, and ran down the sides of his cheeks parallel to his beard line, then back up across the wide, flat bridge of his nose. He was bare chested. The dark skin on his torso, his arms, and his legs were partially painted white to resemble feathers.

Suddenly, from behind the curtain came a troupe of Aborigine entertainers bursting onto the dance floor. Some twirled flaming torches. Others held drums and beat them to the rhythm of the didgeridoo.

Sam watched in amazement and Brit was beside herself with delight.

"This is great, Brit," Sam told her. "Your dad is something else."

"I know he is, Sam'o," Brit smiled. "The dance is called 'The Dreaming.' The group travels the whole of Australia performing it. Through song and dance they tell their history," Brit said, still smiling.

One performer wore a bright red loin cloth and his body was solidly painted pasty white. His eyes were colored with orange and purple pigment. Two young Aborigine girls rushed forward and anointed him with a liquid mixture. Then one of the torch bearers set the man ablaze. The crowd gasped then went wild with cheers and applause. Everyone was astounded as the burning tribesman danced with abandon around the promenade. Every step, every movement was choreographed perfectly to the music.

The show lasted nearly an hour. The music and dancing never stopped and the songs were translated from Aborigine tongue to English. The songs told of all creation, the "Dreamtime," and of the "Creation Ancestors," the "Givers of Dreams."

The troupe exited as rapidly as they entered. There was a long standing ovation when the dancers disappeared behind the curtain. Applause lingered as Wilton moved to Brit's outstretched arms. Sam smiled. Again, he had to.

"Oh, daddy...you don't know what that meant to me. It was the best wedding present of all."

"There's just one more," Wilton said, stepping back and smiling.

Brit's face beamed as she saw, standing behind Wilton, the most ancient of Aborigine, Eloi Unaipon.

He wore a shock of long white hair and a full white beard. His traditional breast-plate signified his position of great rank in his village. His shirt was colorful with one empty sleeve. Eloi held out his one arm, and at once, Brit was there in a fond and tearful embrace.

After a moment Sam and Wilton joined Brit and Eloi. Brit wiped her eyes and said, "Sam'o, this is Eloi. I've known him longer than I can remember."

"It is good I am allowed to meet you, Mister Sam-Sir," Eloi said, reaching to clasp Sam's hand. "Mister Wilton-Sir has said many good things about you. He say you are good for Brittan-ni-Ma'am."

Eloi looked deeply into Sam's eyes, into his heart. There was an uncanny sensation when Sam felt Eloi peering into the marrow. Then, satisfied with what he saw, Eloi smiled.

"Mister Wilton-Sir is right. You are a good man. May He who gives us dreams bless you both this day and for all days to come."

Wilton and Eloi walked away while Brit looked after them. Feeling a little drained, Sam shook his head and said, "Quite a guy."

"Yes," Brit replied, absently. "When I was a little girl his wife would attend me whenever daddy was away on business. When she died, Eloi felt responsible for me from that day on. I owe him my life."

"How's that?"

Brit looked thoughtfully a moment then explained. Wilton had been conducting research on poisonous reptiles for the zoo. He'd gone to the vast flood plains of western Queensland to capture a male and a female inland taipan. The zoo wanted them for breeding stock as well as for study. Brit and Eloi accompanied him on the field trip.

The inland taipan was by far the most deadly land snake in the world. Its dose of neurotoxin was estimated to be fifty times more lethal than that of the Indian cobra, Naja naja. The poison acted swiftly and symptoms included vomiting, flaccid paralysis, and soon thereafter, respiratory paralysis.

Wilton awoke early that morning and took the Jeep deep into the bush. The previous day he'd captured a female snake and he'd gone to try and find a male. Eloi and Brit remained behind to break camp in preparation for their return trip to Brisbane.

They were going to fetch a bucket of water to douse the campfire when Brit nearly stepped on the very serpent Wilton was outback seeking. Eloi grabbed Brit and pulled her backwards to safety. When he did, the snake came and struck Eloi's left arm just above the wrist.

"My God," exclaimed Sam. "Then what happened?"

"It was the most horrible day of my life. I've nearly blotted it out altogether. I suppose that's why I've never told you of it." Brit's eyes told the terror while she recounted the nightmare.

Wilton had taken the vial of antitoxin with

him. Without the antitoxin, death was a certainty, save immediate amputation. Without
pause, Brit, a mere child of twelve, answered
Eloi's acute plea and saved his life. She raised
his machete high above her head, and with all
her might, brought down the blade and severed
his arm at the elbow.

The bleeding was profuse and the pain
intolerable. First Brit made a tourniquet of
hemp and sack cloth. She broadcast the international distress signal and radioed her father
who was two hours away. She then lay beside
her friend to comfort him while he suffered.
When the chills came, the warmth of her body
gave him consolation. He was in deep shock
when the helicopter arrived.

Sam was speechless as Brit folded into his
arms. Then she looked at Sam behind a gentle
smile. "I guess you could say, although under
different circumstances, Eloi is my Mister
Willie."

Sam nodded understandingly and held her
in his arms. Brit was crying but she wasn't
sad.

By eleven o'clock the record crowd had
largely thinned. Charlie and Hat Man were
packing their equipment into the Chevy van
they'd leased from Rooster's Come and Get It

car rental agency. Mister Willie and Eloi were
sitting at the tiki bar, fascinated by one another.
Brit smiled as she watched their lively conversation.

"I suppose they've quite a lot to talk
about," said Brit.

"Yeah," Sam replied. "I'm sure they have.
I wonder if they're having any problem commu-
nicating."

"I suppose not," Brit shrugged. "They
seem to be getting on very well. Sam'o, it's been
a long day. We've got a date. Let's go home."

"I've got a surprise for you, baby," he said
reaching for the key to the lighthouse."

"What's that Sam'o?" She smiled and took
his hand.

"Something special, come on and you'll
see," he said, leading her to her station wagon.
"Maybe we can get out of here before anyone
notices."

The grounds at the Tybee Light Station
were deserted when the newlyweds arrived. At
the North Beach Grill, just east of Tybee Light,
several patron's cars were scattered about the
parking lot, but mostly, all was quiet.

"What are we doing here, luv?," she asked
with an excited gleam in her eye. "Have you
been talking to daddy? You *have* been talking

to him, haven't you?"

"It's ours for the night, lover," he said, stepping out of the station wagon.

Sam walked around the car and opened the door for Brit, reached for her hand, and helped her to her feet. She held Sam a moment and smiled with excitement.

"Just a moment, luv. There's something I have to get from the back seat," Brit opened the car door, reached in, and retrieved a package the size of a shoe box wrapped in red foil paper.

"What's that," Sam asked.

"Something very special," she said and took Sam's hand.

They walked briskly toward the lighthouse. Once inside, an eerie feeling of isolation overtook them as the massive door closed behind. When they began their climb up the cast iron, spiral steps, the March wind whistled and moaned and ghosts of antiquity loomed about the mammoth brick and iron edifice.

When they reached the top landing, their legs were weary from the climb. When Brit stepped inside the watch room gallery, just underneath the lantern chamber, her eyes lit with delight. Sam smiled when she saw what Wilton had prepared.

There was a goose-down mattress with two

pillows and a blanket. Beside the mattress was Sam's ghetto blaster and a stack of cassette tapes. Atop a shiny steel table was a white chenille cloth and a flickering hurricane lamp. Beside the lamp sat a flat silver tray with a bed if ice containing twenty-four giant prawns. Two long stemmed crystal glasses were turned upside down and sitting beside a bottle of Dom Perignon '85 that rested in a silver and gold bucket of ice.

"Oh Sam'o," she rushed to his arms. "Will the surprises never end?"

"Never my love. I promise you that."

Sam kissed her, then went to the table and poured the champagne. Brit set her package on the table, accepted the glass and awaited Sam's toast.

"To you, my lovely wife, and to years of happiness we'll share," they clinked their glasses and drank a swallow.

"I have another surprise for you, baby," Sam reached into his pocket for the locket and put it in her hand.

"It's beautiful, Sam'o," she said with a smile.

"Open it up," Sam said anxiously.

She opened the locket and for a long while there was silence while Brit was lost in the picture. She looked at Sam and wiped her eyes.

"I...I don't know what to say, Sam'o, except thank you. I'll cherish it forever."

Again there was silence as they held one another. After a time, Brit moved from Sam and back to the table. She reached for the package and handed it to him.

"Here, luv, this is for you."

Sam carefully unwrapped the package and neatly folded the paper. He laid the paper on the table and opened the box. Inside was a unique bronze figurine. The statue was the likeness of a raging bull. Lying on her back, lashed to the bull's withers, was a beautiful, terrified, naked woman. A man in a loin cloth held the bull by the horns. He was desperately trying to drag the bull to the ground.

"It's beautiful," Sam said, admiring the intricate artwork.

"When I saw it, I saw you, Sam'o. I saw us both," said Brit.

"I'm not quite sure I understand," Sam smiled back at her, looking puzzled.

"I saw me tied to the bull, a prisoner of my past. I was afraid to feel, afraid to touch, afraid to be touched. Sam'o, I was afraid to love you," Brit looked toward Sam sincerely.

"You knew the depth of my torment," she

went on. "But you loved me anyway and fought to free me. Regardless of the giant you had to slay, you went against it, and you prevailed. You dragged the bull to its knees and set me free. You gave me my wings and let me soar. I love you for that."

"What a beautiful thought," Sam was moved and a single tear fell from his eye. At the time, when he'd given up and walked away, he didn't know he'd mortally wounded the beast that had beset her.

"Now, let me make a toast to you," Brit said raising her glass.

"To you, my wonderful and loving husband. And to the happiness the many years will surely bring."

After the toast, they embraced, and again the world was solely theirs. And once more they thanked their Creator for the love of one another.

After a few minutes, they went to the observation deck. The view at night was spectacular. A ledge directly underneath the light cast a shadow over the deck where they stood. Once again, Sam raised his glass and clinked it against Brit's.

"To us, Brit. I wouldn't trade one minute with you for everything below us."

"To us, Sam'o," she retorted, clinking her glass against his again. "I don't know what we've done to deserve all this. But I'm surely thankful for it."

They made love that night, in the shadows of the watch room gallery underneath hundreds of thousands of candle powers, radiated by the Tybee Light. When they awoke, the Atlantic was just giving birth to a fiery, red ball of morning sun. They gathered their things and made their way back to their condo. No one was the wiser for it.

41

Wilton left for Brisbane the week after the wedding. Before leaving he had one final gift for Brit and Sam: an extended visit to Australia when the couple's work schedule would allow it.

Spring came, and with it, the promise of life re-born. Brit gave her notice and resigned her position at the Shipwreck to help Sam run his plumbing company. By August, the business had grown and Sam had more work than he could do.

Clyde's job was in the final stages of completion. Clyde had bought another tract of land on the middle of the island and plans were being drawn for another project. Despite the success of Sam's business, moving to Brisbane looked more inviting every day. Sam was irritated with the inspections department, and dismayed by the lack of knowledge of many who called themselves builders.

It never made sense that the three primary building trades were required to hold state licenses and take hours of continuing education every year when anyone with the fee to buy a business license could call himself a general contractor. Moreover, why weren't the general contractors required to pass the rigorous examinations like the tradesmen? After all, the contractors were the ones ultimately in charge of the projects. South Carolina and Florida required contractors to be licensed through the state. Why didn't Georgia?

It would really be nice, thought Sam, if he lived in a land where he'd never again see a friend's home and life ruined because of shoddy work. A workplace without the Shaneekas and the Clovis Larks would be a safer workplace indeed.

Brit was Sam's refuge. When he came home in the evenings, dusted off his feet at the door and smelled supper on the stove, nothing else really mattered. Brit only worked half-days so she spent her afternoons as she chose. She'd bought a potter's wheel, became good with clay, and displayed her creations at the Nautilus Studio Gallery on the north end of the island. Brit's life was joyous and peaceful. She was proud of Sam, and Sam took pride in that fact. He was fulfilled because he could give her the life that she loved.

By the last week of August, provisions had been made for Jerry to take over all business operations while Sam and Brit vacationed in Australia. Wilton had planned several unique surprises for them upon their arrival. Autumn on Tybee was spring down under and the weather was fine. The couple would touch down in Brisbane the seventh of September.

42

The eve before the couple's departure, Brit was busy packing and making last-minute preparations. Sam worked hard tying up loose ends on several jobs nearing completion.

Brit could hardly wait for her husband to see Queensland, the Sunshine State. Brisbane, the state's capital, enjoyed the world's finest climate for outdoor living, just the climate Sam

would love. He'd be amazed at the vivid, tropical beauty and bold, rich colors, magnified by
brilliant sunshine.

It will be so romantic, she thought, seeing
him there when the sun goes down and turns
the city's towers to copper and gold, and the
shimmer of the Brisbane River's beauty reflects
in his eyes. She'd take him down the Gold Coast
to the lorikeet feedings at Currunbin Sanctuary. He'll love the breathtaking scenery at
Numinbah Valley and the spectacle of
Purlinbrook Falls, cascading a hundred ninety
meters, to the rocks below.

She could almost feel his touch when
they'd soon be making love in the dry eucalypt
bushland, and by a stream in the lush, sub-
tropical rainforest on Mount Glorious. Sam
laughed when she told him of the giant, green
tree-frogs that would probably be watching them
in their fanciful jungle retreat. He could nearly
smell the jacarandas, bougainvillea, wattles,
bauhinias and other spectacular flowering trees
she'd told him of. Best of all there'd be the loving he'd promised in Platypus Bay.

Their excitement nearly preempted sleep
that night and it was almost one o'clock before
they drifted away to slumber. The next day
would be a long one because their flight wasn't

scheduled to leave Savannah until five-twenty in the afternoon. Sam was lying there watching it all come alive before his eyes when the telephone rang and stole his dream. Sleepily, he rolled over and picked up the receiver.

"Hello," he managed, wondering who would possibly be calling.

"Sam," an urgent voice came over the line. "This is Otho Sthathopoulos and I've got an emergency."

Otho owned a large beachfront motel on the south end of the island and was one of Sam's valued customers. Sam tried to be polite but failed.

"Damn, Otho. Do you have any idea what time it is?"

"I know it's late, Sam, and I apologize. I called your twenty-four hour emergency number, and I guess it rolled over to you're phone."

Now Sam was irritated at himself. In all the rush he forgot to change call forwarding to the plumber who was on call that night. Whose bright idea was it to offer twenty-four hour emergency service anyway, he thought.

"All right, Otho," Sam said reluctantly. "What's the problem?"

"Some drunk shot off a pistol in the hallway down at my motel and the bullet punctured

the main water line. There is inches of water in
my lobby and nobody there knows how to shut
it off."

"Stay calm, Otho, I'm on the way." Sam
hung up the phone and turned toward Brit.

"Shall I go with you, Sam'o?" she asked.

"No, baby, it's nasty out," he said, listening to the wind rattle the windows. "Tomorrow
is a big day and you're exhausted from packing. You get some sleep and I'll be home as
soon as I can."

"I hate for you to have to go out in this
weather but I love you for doing it," she said.

"It's my own fault, Brit. My grandmother
tried to tell me. Be a doctor, be a lawyer, be an
Indian Chief. Be anything but a plumber. Did I
listen? Hell no, I didn't listen and this is what I get."

"Oh Sam'o, don't be so dramatic," Brit
laughed and playfully pushed him. "I really don't
mind riding with you, you know."

"That's okay, baby. It's late and it's going
to storm." Sam threw on his clothes, kissed
her good-bye, and was off to quell the panic.

43

On the second floor of the "A" building, at
the north end of the Tybee Island Beach Resort,

a young woman threw her laundry into one of the recently installed clothes dryers. She was glad for the new washers and dryers because, even at two in the morning, the old ones were usually occupied. More than 200 families lived in the "A" building and many people worked late, so it was necessary for them to do laundry in the wee hours. She dropped seventy-five cents into the slots, pushed in the mechanism, and the dryer tumbled on. She returned to her condo to wait the forty minutes it would take for her clothes to dry.

The electrical wire that was run from the panel box to the three-hole, two-forty volt receptacle was too small for the load. The circuit breaker it ran from was too large. The heavy duty commercial dryer had been in operation only ten minutes before the insulation melted off the wire. Inside the wall, just below the county inspection sticker, a bolt of electricity arced and set the paper-backed fiberglass insulation ablaze. The flames quickly spread and ignited the indoor-outdoor carpet in the laundry room. A strong northeast wind rushed down the hallway and fanned the fire.

Instantly, the room was engulfed in searing heat. The flames licked the dry, plywood ceiling, and within minutes, the corridor and the eastern, exterior walls of the building were being consumed by the fire's insatiable hunger. After the second floor ceiling gave way, the fierce heat began to devour the undersized, structural members that supported the floor above.

The fire jumped up the walls and raged southward down the third-floor hallway. Simultaneously, it rose up the outer walls, swallowed the second and third-floor balconies, and flanked the residences as it roared southward down the complex. The heat in the corridor was so intense, the paint on Brit's front door bubbled.

Many men, women, and children died at the north end of the building before the fire alarm sounded and Brit awoke. Between the deafening blasts of the alarm, she heard the roaring fire. There was screaming, begging, pleading, and cries of terror. Brit jumped from her bed, threw on her kimono and ran for the front door. When she touched the metal, the fleshy palm of her hand burned like meat on a hot griddle. She tore her hand away, leaving a smoldering patch of skin on the door. Before the pain, came the sickening, sweet smell of her own burning flesh.

The rope! She remembered the nylon rope. Sam had tied a rope to the rail and left it coiled on the back porch for just such a time. He'd made a way for her escape! She ran down the hall toward the balcony. As she passed the kitchen, the glass, patio door imploded and fire burst through, blocking her exit. Thick, black smoke surged skyward behind billowing, yellow flames.

She ran back to the bedroom and looked through the window, into the corridor. The area was the same, nowhere to run, nowhere to hide. The heat was unbearable, and the breath she gasped for, blistering and foreboding.

She went to the bathroom and shut both doors. In darkness, she felt her way to the lavatory and found the candle she always lit before she had her bath. She found her matches and lit the candle. She opened the tub faucet and wet two bath towels. She pressed them under the cracks at the bottom of the doors and sat on the floor with her candle.

"Please God, don't let me burn alive," she prayed, crying into folded hands.

She sat watching the flickering candle flame become smaller as the oxygen in the bathroom was depleted. The candle flickered one last time and the sweltering heat faded away. In her mind's eye, she held Sam's hand as they plunged together into the cool, clear waters of

Platypus Bay. Her prayer was answered as she drifted into unconsciousness.

44

Sam made a temporary patch of rubber gasket material and wrapped it around the three-inch copper water line. The bullet just grazed the pipe but it knocked a hole in it the size of a dime. The next day, Otho could call the shop and have a permanent repair made, but the temporary fix would get him through the night.

After securing the patch with two stainless-steel hose clamps, he proceeded to the mechanical room. He turned the wheel atop the iron-bodied gate valve and water rushed into the pipes. After a few moments, the gushing sound abated, then there was silence.

While walking down the hall toward the site of the repair, he thought perhaps this would be the last time he'd ever be called in the middle of the night to take care of a plumbing problem. He might just stay in Brisbane and find something else to do. The prospect brought a smile to his lips. He climbed the ladder with his flashlight and examined the surety of the temporary patch. He was pleased to find that the patch was holding and he could go home and crawl back into bed.

As he slid the last new acoustic ceiling tile into its track, he heard a police siren screaming north down Butler Avenue. Judging by the strident sound of the siren, he thought the cruiser must have been traveling ninety miles an hour.

He returned the ladder to the storage room and locked the door behind him. He was pleased that the service-call went well. He'd only been gone an hour and forty-five minutes. If the bullet had ripped the pipe apart, it could've been an all-night job. While walking back to the front desk, he heard fire trucks racing past the motel, horns blowing, sirens howling.

When he reached the lobby, the night auditor was gone. Impatiently, he waited for her return, so he could let her know the repair had been made, and the water supply was back in service. Momentarily, she burst through the front door, looking astonished. Her eyes were wildly excited when she confronted him.

"Quick," she said. "Come look. The sky is on fire!"

Sam followed her into the parking lot. The woman was hysterical as she grabbed him and pointed toward the sky. The sky indeed appeared aflame. It looked as if a bomb had hit the north end of the island. The night was bright orange.

Sam ran for his truck. The tires squealed as he rounded the corner onto Butler Avenue. He ignored the stoplight at Fourteenth Street, and floored the accelerator. By the time he made the big curve just north of the DeSoto, his fears were all but confirmed. There were only four structures on the north end large enough to fuel such a fire: The Savannah Beach and Racquet Club, Lighthouse Point, Clyde's job, and the Tybee Island Beach Resort.

Five more fire trucks came from Thunderbolt and Savannah. As Sam raced home, he saw them turn left, sirens shrieking, horns blowing, onto Beach Resort Drive. Three police cars lined up, one behind the other, and blocked the roadway. Sam slammed on the brakes and the truck screeched to a halt, just inches from Billy Braxton's police cruiser. Sam jumped from the truck and ran over where Billy and two other officers were standing. At that instant, the sky opened, and torrential rain poured down drenching them all.

"Have you seen Brittany?" Sam shouted through the noise.

"Just a minute," Billy responded, reaching into his cruiser for his rain gear.

"I don't have a minute," Sam yelled and grabbed Billy's arm.

Billy averted his eyes and searched for a way to tell him. "I don't know if she made it out," he said, pulling on his raincoat.

Sam started to run toward the building but Billy and the other two officers caught him. Frantically, he struggled to break free, but they had him down.

"There's nothing you can do for her," Billy shouted through the drumming torrents. "You'll only get in the way of the firemen."

"Okay, okay, Billy," Sam said. "I'm calm now. I'm all right."

When Sam stopped struggling, the officers released him. In a flash Sam bolted past them and ran between the police cars to find his wife. When he saw the burning building and felt the heat, all hopes of finding her alive were gone with the smoke. He dropped to his knees, clinched his fists, and looked toward the heavens.

"Why...God...why?" Sam wailed. He fell on his face, pounded his fist into the mud, and he wept.

45

At six o'clock that morning Sam ran through the emergency entrance at the Savannah Trauma Center. He was soaking wet and covered in mud. The hospital was full of medical staff who were trying to help those who survived the fire and consoling the friends and relatives of those who hadn't.

Frantically, Sam searched for Doctor Angus O'Leary, Sam's and Brit's family physician who practiced on Tybee. Brit was found alive. But Sam knew little else.

The fireman who climbed through the roof and carried Brit out told Sam she was unconscious when he brought her down and laid her on the stretcher. The only visible burn she'd suffered was on her hand. He'd said that Brit was the last one rescued before the rescue effort was abandoned. He told Sam that Life Star helicopter had taken her to the center.

At eight-thirty the doctor sent a nurse to tell Sam that he was attending Brit. The nurse brought some medication the doctor prescribed for Sam to help him cope. She told Sam the doctor would see him soon.

It was another hour before Sam saw the doctor walk through the swinging doors and into the waiting room. Doctor O'Leary stared blankly at the floor as he approached. Many who died or were maimed that morning were his patients and his friends. His eyes were bloodshot and his face was flushed. He was exhausted. Sam jumped from his chair and ran his way.

"She's alive but her condition is critical," Doctor O'Leary said, with his strong Irish accent. His voice trembled.

"Can I see her?" Sam's lips quivered, his eyes filled with tears.

"Come, Sam, sit down with me."

The doctor placed a gentle hand on Sam's shoulder and coaxed him toward the couch. When they were seated, he took Sam's hands in his own with a look of compassion.

"Is she going to be all right?" Sam asked.

"We don't know, Sam."

Sam winced, wiped his eyes and stared out the window.

"Can I see her?"

"She's in intensive care. I can't let you go in muddy like you are. She wouldn't know you were there anyway. She hasn't regained consciousness. We have her on a respirator."

Sam hung his head into his hands and he cried. Doctor O'Leary put his arm around Sam and tried to comfort him. When Sam collected himself the doctor spoke.

"Go back to Tybee. They've set up a shelter in Memorial Park near the library. They'll have some clothes for you. Take your medication, take a hot bath, and try to get some rest."

"When can I see her?"

"Come back tonight. We're going to do some tests. We'll know more then."

46

The stop light at Waters Avenue and Victory Drive seemed stuck on red. When the light turned green, Sam's thoughts were miles away. The driver behind him sounded his horn and swore, which brought Sam back from his stupor.

The stretch of highway between the town of Thunderbolt and Tybee Island was squalling with sirens. The sky thundered with medi-vac helicopters from Hunter Army Air Field and the Savannah Trauma Center. Traffic was backed up for miles and the journey home seemed endless.

The Lazaretto Creek Bridge was check point Alpha. Only island residents, emergency personnel, and the news media were allowed on the Island. Even with all the turmoil, the drive to Tybee was a blur to Sam. He was little more than a zombie, as pain gave way to nothingness.

The emergency shelter at Memorial Park was over crowded and under staffed. There were two long, green, Army tents pitched parallel to Butler Avenue. Under the tents were tables stacked with clothing and food. The items were donated by the Salvation Army and were flown in from the mainland by military transport.

A row of chemical toilets sat beside refugee tents where temporary quarters were established. Little children wailed for their mothers, some of whom never answered. Many suffered from smoke inhalation. Some were burned and awaited medical attention. Others were merely homeless and mortified at the spectacle.

One little girl had torn her clothes off. Her back had been burned but not so severely as others. The scene was reminiscent of a photograph Sam remembered from 1972. A young South Vietnamese girl was running down a road screaming. She had torn her flaming clothes from her body after being napalmed in error by a South Vietnamese warplane.

Memorial Park looked like a combat zone. Only the dead were without supplication. A lone tent at the southwest corner of the park housed them. Some wore identification tags tied to their toes. Most were burned beyond recognition. The smell of death overwhelmed the breath of the sea.

Sam wandered through the mire, unsure whether he was there to seek comfort or to give it. Suddenly, he was brought around by a tap on his shoulder. Sam looked behind him and into a T.V. news camera. A reporter held a microphone in his hand and confronted Sam.

"Excuse me, Mister Lewis. I was told that you are a resident at the Beach Resort. I'm Lindsey Buckner from WTJS Television. Would you care to comment on this calamity?"

"I...I've never seen anything like it. I never saw a building go up so fast," Sam responded in a daze.

"Do you know what started the fire?" the anchor man pressed on.

"You'll...you'll have to excuse me, Mister Buckner, I've had a...a long night."

Lindsey Buckner signaled the camera man to pan over the crowd and away from him and Sam. Lindsey turned off his microphone and removed a business card from his pocket.

"There's more here than meets the eye, Mister Lewis, a lot more." He handed the card to Sam with a cold stare.

"You're right, Mister Buckner, there is. But I can't think about it right now. My wife...she...she's."

"I know, Mister Lewis. Our prayers are with her. When things settle down, call me, please." Something in Lindsey's eyes told more than his words that day.

47

It was 11 A.M. before Jerry found Sam wandering near Memorial Park. Jerry had been waiting at the Trauma Center when, by chance, he ran into Doctor O'Leary. The doctor told Jerry of Brit's condition and told him he'd probably find Sam at the shelter.

Earlier that morning, Jerry was awakened by fire trucks screaming across the Lazaretto Creek Bridge. When he walked out onto the deck of his Hatteras, he saw the fire in the eastern sky. When Jerry learned that the "A" building was destroyed and Brit was hospitalized, he called Brisbane.

Wilton phoned his old friend and comrade in arms, Lord Huntington, the Royal Australian Air Marshall. Lord Huntington made the necessary arrangements between the Australian and American military, and within two hours,

Wilton was bound for America at twice the speed of sound.

Jerry saw Sam wandering down Butler Avenue by the park, still covered in mud, and looking hopeless and lost. When Jerry hailed him, and Sam started for the Mercedes, Sam's expression was detached. He didn't acknowledge Jerry when he opened the passenger door and got in.

"Let's get you to the boat, buddy," Jerry told him. "A hot shower and some dry clothes will do you good," Jerry said, prodding Sam for a reaction.

When they reached the Lazaretto Creek Marina, Jerry pulled into his parking spot. He looked over at Sam, who was staring through the windshield. Jerry got out, walked around the car and opened the passenger door. Without a word, Sam got out of the Mercedes, walked past the marina, past the Cafe Loco, down the ramp, and to the long floating dock. Jerry watched Sam as he followed him at a respectable distance. Sam boarded the boat, entered the cabin and slid shut the door behind him.

When Jerry stepped on board, he heard water running in the shower by the head in the main berth. Jerry put on a pot of coffee, laid some clothes on the bed for Sam, and waited.

After a time, Sam emerged from the cabin, clothed, clean of mud, but still without expression.

"I talked to Doctor O'Leary," said Jerry, searching for any sign. "Her condition is stable but her lungs are in pretty bad shape."

Jerry went to the counter, poured a mug of black coffee, and handed it to Sam. Sam walked to the port side of the boat, propped his foot on the railing, and watched some children on the other side of the creek crabbing with frayed string tied to a chicken neck.

"I called Wilton," said Jerry. "He'll be landing at Hunter Army Airfield this evening."

For a long while there was silence. Sam continued fixed on the children. He fumbled for a pack of cigarettes lying next to a lighter on the boat's console. He lit up and took a long draw. He sipped his coffee, eyed the cigarette, then threw it into the creek.

"Brit is always after me to quit these damn things. She says she hopes I come to my senses before it's too late," Jerry listened as Sam continued.

"She says smoking cigarettes makes me smell something like a goat. But she says you can't help who you fall in love with. So what's a shiela to do?"

The children laughed as they contended with a particularly disagreeable blue crab they'd landed.

"I can't wait to see her tonight," said Sam, "so I can tell her I've decided to quit. She'll be happy to hear that. You know she could always beat me on a breath-hold dive," Sam rambled on. "But it's only because of cigarettes," Sam turned up his mug and drank the last swallow.

"Remember the time Brit and I took the boat out by ourselves? You'd gone to town or some damn where. We anchored on a ledge in eighty feet of water. I put on my gear and went down the anchor line alone to see if there was anything worth diving on. I barely reached the ocean floor before I felt a tap on my shoulder. I turned around and it was Brit. And you know what?" Sam glanced at Jerry. "She wasn't wearing scuba gear," said Sam.

"She took the regulator from my mouth and took a breath off it. She gave me a kiss and said 'I love you, Sam'o.' Then she gave me back my regulator and swam for the surface," Sam smiled.

"She said I love you, huh?" Jerry smiled back.

Jerry re-filled Sam's coffee cup then Sam sat at the little table opposite Jerry. Sam looked back across the creek and the children were gone. Then he spoke with a smile and a tear.

"Yeah. That's what she said. It was the first time she ever told me. Her voice was garbled when it came through the water. But I knew what she said."

48

At six o'clock that evening a United States Army Black Hawk helicopter touched down on the landing pad atop the Savannah Trauma Center. The door opened and Wilton Hayes jumped from the gun ship. He leaned over as he trotted under the rotor blades and to an open door where Doctor Isadore Goldstein was waiting.

Doctor Goldstein was a respiratory specialist. Some forty years earlier, after graduating Emory University Medical School, magna cum laude, Doctor Goldstein began his internship at New York's Mount Sinai Hospital. It was there he learned the downside of his calling. That night, he would again wonder if the rewards were worth the anguish. Wilton listened while Doctor Goldstein talked.

He told him that Brit's lungs were seared, perhaps irreversibly. She had inhaled massive

amounts of smoke that caused oxygen depriva-
tion to the brain. An E.E.G. had revealed little
neurological activity and paralysis to all quad-
rants of her body was a certainty. Only a respirator kept Brit breathing and her life hung in
the balance.

Both lungs had been catheterized to prevent her drowning from exudation into the pleu-
ral cavities. She was given intravenous fluids
to avert dehydration and a continuous flow of
antibiotics to ward off infections.

Wilton followed the doctor down the stair-
case, through a corridor, and to the elevator.
On their way to the third floor and to the Intensive Care Unit, Wilton was reminded of the night
Brittany was born, the night he lost his wife. It
was a dismal evening, a world away, and eons
past.

He remembered the hospital walls, in-
stitutional green and cold as an earthen grave.
He thought of Gloria's smile the first time she
heard her baby cry, the last time she heard
her cry. Then Gloria's body relaxed. Her eyes
waxed empty, and her stare became fixed and
dilated. Wilton closed her eyes, kissed her
away, and she gave up the ghost. A chill overtook him when he knew he was alone, alone
to raise the child.

The tiny hand clinged for life to his finger, a glimmer of light on a night so alone. Those sweet little eyes he'd always remember. And twilight's repose gave him strength to go on.

Wilton remembered her first birthday and her pretty blue dress with her crinolines billowing in the cool Brisbane breeze. His eyes tried to smile but his heart sent only tears.

He'd held her hand again, not so long ago, and prayed for her deliverance when she lay unconscious from the beating. He prayed he might peer into the eyes of the jackal who'd hurt her. And he prayed that worm might know who'd spilled his blood before he reached his realm eternal.

The last time he'd held her hand was a joyous time. It was the time he passed that hand to Sam for his love and for his keeping. Soon, he'd hold her hand once more. And this time he thought, perhaps, for the last time.

At six-thirty Sam and Jerry arrived at the Trauma Center. Just before leaving Tybee, Sam spoke with the charge nurse on duty at the Intensive Care Unit. He'd been in nearly constant contact with I.C.U. since Jerry picked him up near Memorial Park earlier in the day.

When they walked through the double stainless steel doors at the Trauma Center's

I.C.U., they were met by Wilton and Doctor
Goldstein. Wilton cried as he held Sam and
whispered. "She didn't know who I was, Sam'o.
She didn't even know I was there."

"I'm sorry to tell you, son," the doctor said
to Sam. "But it would take a miracle. We've
done all we can do. So be prepared."

When Sam walked into the room and saw
her, he never knew such helplessness, such
hopelessness. All that was his he would have
given, had her plight been a mere bewitching, a
prick of a spinning needle, a spell to be broken
with only a kiss.

Sam walked to her side, took her hand in
his, and went to his knees. As tears flowed, he
prayed. "Dear God. If there is any way, take
this cup from this beautiful soul. If it's a life
you want, and if I'm at all worthy, make her
whole, Lord, and take me in her place."

49

Sam sat on the floor in his cabana drinking cheap whiskey straight out of the bottle. He
was staring at the bronze figurine Brit had given
him. Brit was gone, and the figurine was all
that was left. Somehow it had come through
the fire unscathed. Officer Billy Braxton had

retrieved it from the ruins and had given it back to Sam. Beside the statue sat a silver urn. Engraved on the urn was the same inscription etched in the wedding ring, still on his finger: God Is Love.

Sam remembered the first time he ever saw her, that wonderful smile, the precious laughter. He thought of the first kiss in the blue gondola, high above Tybrisa Street, high atop the Ferris wheel. And he remembered that first night in the cabana when he knew her completely. The touch of her hand. The warmth of her body. Her kiss.

All things come to pass, thought Sam. Nothing comes to stay. Sam didn't recall what day he decided to quit blaming himself for what happened to Brit. He only knew he had. Or had he? He'd once read that woulda, coulda, shoulda thinking was a self-destructive process. And it nearly destroyed Sam Lewis.

Twice, the night of the fire, Brit asked Sam to go with him and twice he turned her down. If he'd only taken her along she would still have been alive. Or would she? You come into this world with a way to go out, reasoned Sam. That thought alone saved his sanity. Or did it?

A lot of things had happened since Sam lost his wife. Some good. Some bad. Mostly bad. Tom Marshall finally found some peace after they let him out of the state mental hospital. But he still kept a picture of Jan hanging on his wall.

Hat Man and Charlie began playing their music more frequently together. And Charlie was getting good at playing the didgeridoo Wilton had sent him. They were playing at Doc's Bar one night when a recording executive from Nashville walked right in and discovered them. The first compact disk that hit the market went platinum in record tempo. Sometimes good things happen to good people, thought Sam.

They condemned the old water tower and built a new one. They needed a new water tower. Tybee Island water smelled pretty rotten.

Kareem went to work for Morrison Mechanical, a crackerjack plumbing and heating company in Savannah. They accepted him into their apprenticeship program and he was named rookie of the year. Indeed, he'd learned to keep the bubble between the lines.

They auctioned off the rides from the amusement park and built a motel where the rides once stood. Sam tried to buy the blue gondola, the one where he sat with Brit when they first kissed, but the owner sold the whole wheel to a used car dealership instead.

Clyde sold his house on Tybee and moved back to Augusta because he couldn't build a quality product and compete with the shoddy contractors. He was disillusioned by the Inspections Department and fed up with the whole damned mess.

Sam hadn't seen Jerry since he cranked up his boat and floated away. And some developer thought it'd be a neat idea to tear down the DeSoto and build condominiums.

Sam's business had failed. It slid right out of his fingers, right into the dumper. But Sam didn't care. He never really even noticed. He was too busy trying to bring sight to the blind and make the deaf hear. But the blind wouldn't look and the deaf didn't listen. At least that was the way Sam saw it. At least that was the way he remembered it. He wasn't sure.

Sam did remember the day he went crazy though. It was the day he learned the Department Of The Treasury's Bureau Of Alcohol, Tobacco, And Firearms declared that, in the area of the fire's origin, wires had burned in two. And indications of arcing were observed at the separated ends. It was the day he learned that Shaneeka Holmes had been the inspector who approved the faulty electrical installation.

It was the day Sam stormed into Tybee

Island City Hall and demanded that Fred Haney, the City Marshall, give account why the installation was not properly inspected by someone with expertise in the electrical field. It was the day Fred Haney showed Sam a building permit that read, "PERMIT HOLDER AGREES TO HOLD THE CITY OF TYBEE ISLAND HARMLESS ON ANY CONSTRUCTION COVERED BY THIS PERMIT." It was the day Fred told Sam that if he had a problem with the disclaimer he could take it up with City Council or tell it to the fuckin' birds.

It was the day he realized nobody gave a shit Brit was dead. And they didn't give a shit that other Brit's were out there dying everyday because nobody gave a shit. The City Council didn't give a shit. The county didn't give a shit. The Tybee code enforcement officials didn't give a shit. And the fuckin' birds didn't give a shit.

Sam remembered the day he started his little war. It was a war with the county and the city of Tybee Island. It was a war he couldn't win. Not that he didn't try. He and Lindsey Buckner of WTJS Television were going to change the world. But all their little war did was get Lindsey killed and send Sammy on the fast track to losing what little grip he had left on reality.

The T.V. station had agreed to set up a bogus construction site, man it with bogus construction workers, and film the incompetent inspections department right in the act of conducting their incompetent inspections.

Sam deliberately put in the plumbing incorrectly. He called the county and voila! Shaneeka passed it lickity split.

Lindsey bought a book on electrical installation at a hardware store, did just the opposite of what the book told him to do, and shazaam! Shaneeka stuck an inspection sticker right square in the panel box.

When time came for the framing inspection, the carpenter deliberately omitted the hurricane clips from the exterior walls, to prove a point, while at the same time he undersized the rafters and ceiling joists. The point was that as far as framing was concerned, all Shaneeka knew to look for were hurricane clips. She caught the hurricane clip infraction and turned down the inspection faster than a speeding bullet. Nope, thought Sam. Old Shaneeka didn't know a chair rail from a piece of quarter round, but she damn well knew a hurricane clip when she saw one.

Everything seemed to be going Sam's way. Everything was caught on film and audio. It was presented to the public on the six o'clock news in a five-day forum called "Inspecting the Inspectors." Yesiree, buddy, Sam figured. He had the county by the balls, and the city of Tybee Island by the short hairs. Until he learned that nobody gave a shit.

The news story did succeed in turning a few heads, though. Jeffery Andrews got off his medication when he learned Sam was trying to get him fired from his job and Lindsey Buckner was in on the scheme. Jeffery walked up to Lindsey and blew his brains out right in front of the Tybee Island City Hall. Jeffery damn well *was* pissed. Then he turned the gun on Sam, pulled the trigger, and missed. When Sam jumped for cover behind the Police Chief's patrol car, Jeffery ran after him. When the cops pulled their guns and ordered Jeffery to freeze, he turned the gun on himself and blew his own shitty brains out.

What a bloody mess, Brit would have said. Yep, thought Sam. That's what Brit would've said all right. Except Brit was dead and nobody gave a shit.

They sent Jeffery's corpse up to Atlanta to the State Crime Lab for an autopsy to find out what killed him. That made a hell of a lot of sense. It made about as much sense as everything else had been making lately. The bastard's brains were scattered all over Butler Avenue, and they packed him up and sent him off to Atlanta to find out why he was dead.

As soon as they figured out he was dead because he blew his own shitty brains out, they promoted Shaneeka to Chief Inspector and Brit was dead and nobody gave a shit.

Just when Sam made up his mind that life wasn't fit for living, a knock came on the door. Sam stood from the floor and looked out the window at the police cars. He saw Sergeant Billy Braxton and two rookie cops in their blue uniforms with their badges and their guns and told them to go fuck themselves. Sam had boarded himself up in the cabana and he wasn't moving.

"You've gotta come out of there, Sam," said Billy as he peered through the window that Sam had carefully boarded up. The two huge trac hoes were rumbling toward the cabana and they rattled the ground as they came. The news writer would subsequently call them front end loaders. Dumb bastard didn't know a front end loader from a trac hoe. Hell, thought Sam. Maybe *he'd* make a good inspector one day.

G.D. Striker, a wealthy developer from Carolina, had purchased the DeSoto property with the intention of building a stack of expensive condominiums. A gallant effort had been made by the Tybee Island Historical Society and a group of concerned citizens to save the grand old lady, but Striker was unsympathetic to their cause.

The Historical Society offered Striker a price that would have netted him a cool million just for shuffling some papers but he rejected the offer. A second offer was in the works but Striker was in no mood to wait. He began demolition and drove a piling into the ground at the front of the property in defiance of public sentiment.

The entire DeSoto Beach Motel had been gutted and its contents sold at auction. The destruction of the DeSoto started early that morning. First they knocked down the main building that housed the Shipwreck Lounge. They hauled off the ruins with a steady stream of dump trucks as islanders looked on in disbelief. Then came the fall of the Villa Caroline that sat directly beside Butler Avenue.

"You've got to come out of there. Do you hear me, Sam? I know how you feel but you've got to give it up," said Billy.

"Go fuck yourself," Sam yelled again.

"Sam. If I wasn't your friend, I'd haul your

ass outa there and take you to jail for trespass-
ing. Now, come on out."

"Go fuck yourself."

Striker paced impatiently beside the cabana while Billy tried to reason with Sam.
Striker wanted to make damn sure he tore down
the whole kit and caboodle before some other
whacked-out historical conservationist who had
no respect for the meaning of a dollar tried to
get in his way.

"Get him out of there," the demolition foreman yelled at the police. "This is Mister Striker's
property now."

"Look," said Billy. "Don't you care that a
lot of people loved this old place? Doesn't it
even bother you what they think?"

"Mister Striker ain't in this to win friends
and influence people," said the foreman. "Now,
get him out!"

"Listen, pal, please try and understand,"
said Billy. "The man has lost everything he ever
had. He's lost his wife, for God's sake."

"Yeah. Well, cry me a river. Just get him
out of there."

"All right, ass hole," said Billy. "I'll get
him out. But one thing is for sure."

"What's that?"

"You people can't take your money with

you when you go. Can you?"

"Just get him out. It's getting late so get him out now or I'll have your job and I'll sue the city of Tybee Island."

Sam watched as Billy and the rookies went to their police cars and came back with two crow bars and a fire axe. When Billy struck the front door with the first blow of the axe, Sam took down the barricade covering the rear window. He collected his figurine, the urn, a fresh half gallon of whiskey, and crawled out the window. He quickly jumped over the sea wall, and onto the sand just as Billy and the rookie cops broke through the door. Jerry Kirbo silently watched through the darkness as Sam slipped past the wooden ramp, down the beach, and disappeared into the sand dunes.

Sam found a secluded spot in the dunes that suited him and sat on the sand. He examined the badly tarnished figurine, then set it down beside him next to the urn. He opened the whiskey, turned the bottle up, and drank until he gagged.

"Smooth," coughed Sam as he screwed the plastic cap back on the container. He sat and stared at the figurine. He remembered what Brit said when she gave it to him. Yeah, Sam thought. You take the bull by the horns,

don't you, mate?   You really take it by the
fuckin' horns.

By the time the jug of whiskey was half
gone, Sam took the notion to chug down the
balance of the bottle. He didn't know how much
alcohol it would take, or how fast he had to drink
it to poison himself, but he thought it was worth
a shot. He unscrewed the cap and drew a long
swig off the bottle. The whiskey gurgled as it
flowed into his mouth.

What if this doesn't do the trick? I'll find
another way. I'll make one last dive, he thought.
Maybe I can find Jerry and talk him into going
on one more little trip. Maybe I can convince
him to do some blue-water diving at the edge of
the continental shelf, have a little outing at the
Gulf Stream.

"Here's to you, Jeffery Andrews, you crazy
son of a bitch. You brainless Bozo," Sam said,
and took another long swig off his bottle.

He could bail off in a thousand feet of
water, purge the air from his buoyancy control
vest, and float down effortlessly to Davey Jones'
locker, he thought, down to leviathan. At 200
feet, he'd feel just about as nifty as he did right
then. He'd have a whale of a case of nitrogen
narcosis, rapture of the deep, and everything
would be just peachy.

"To you, Clovis Lark, you rotten bastard," Sam was beginning to wobble about and slur his words as the dribble frothed from his mouth. After Clovis ruined the Marshall's house, he and his bumbling son, Clovis Jr., erected a set of shoddy built condos just up the road from where the DeSoto once stood.

During construction, Sam sneaked into the project and photographed the mess the Larks had made. Sam gave copies of photos showing numerous code infractions to the City Marshall but he didn't give a shit. He didn't give a shit when he'd witnessed shoddy built fire walls, structural weakness, and other faults that would compromise the health and safety of future residents.

He didn't give a shit that unlicensed jacklegs were illegally doing plumbing work on Lark's job and all over the island. He didn't give a shit when he knew a jackleg wannabe plumber was installing unsanitary plumbing at the big yellow and blue apartment house on Eighteenth Street. He didn't even give a shit when he knew the Larks were dumping raw sewage into the storm drain behind their shitty project.

He didn't give a shit when Sam told him that a general contractor was wiring a house over on Anderson Court without an electrical contractor's license. And Brit was dead and he didn't give a shit about that either.

At 300 feet, Sam would be disoriented from nitrogen flowing in his blood. At that depth, oxygen toxicity would further contribute to his fine plan. He'd no longer know or care about anything.

"And here's to you, Shaneeka, to your continuing diligence and professionalism. Make sure old Clovis don't fuck things up too bad, will you now."

At 400 feet, if he made it that far, Sam wouldn't know his own name. He wouldn't know who he was or what he was. By then, he'd have forgotten about his wife and there'd be no more pain. He'd have forgotten to equalize the air space in his head, and as he further descended, the pressure would crush his skull. But he wouldn't care. He'd have no more awareness than the mindless fiddler crabs that lived behind his cabana.

"And here's to you, Brit," Sam broke down and wept with total release. "Forgive me, my love," he pleaded convulsively. "Forgive me for letting you down...forgive me for letting you die."

By midnight, the bottle of whiskey was empty, and so was Sam Lewis. The devils

in his head tormented him, even unto unconsciousness.

50

Sam awoke at sun up. Hundreds of tiny
ants crawled over him. They weren't the sting-
ing kind, though. Not the big brown fire ants
that crawled into Texas from South America and
spread all over the south. Those were the Fire
Ants that came out of their mounds by the thousands when someone stepped on them. They
were even known to kill new born cattle and
sheep. Their sting produced an itchy boil filled
with pus. Instead, Sam's tormentors were the
irritating little black ants that worried hell out
of someone when they woke up in the morning
drunk on the beach. Sam lay semiconscious as
he brushed them away.

He detected the sound of a squabble of
laughing gulls sitting in the sand near him. He
opened his eyes and one of the gulls hopped
closer to his head, laughed indignantly, then
hopped back to the safety of its flock.

Sam held the empty whiskey bottle in his
hand. When the gull came forward and laughed
again, Sam threw the bottle at it. The bird side-
stepped the throw, hesitated a moment, cocked

its head, then laughed once more.

Misty rain began to fall. Sam was nauseous and his stomach threatened to turn on him. When his entrails betrayed him, he fell back onto the sand, surrendered to the elements, and wallowed in his misery.

His head pounded and he cursed all creation when he heard bulldozers and trac hoes scraping the ground and removing the remnants of the cabana. Sam just wanted to die. Was that asking too much? Everything he touched turned to naught. He couldn't even drink himself to death. And he couldn't cry anymore. There were no more tears and nothing left to cry over.

Sam drifted in and out until mid-morning. Passersby shook their heads, then walked on. A little girl stopped and teased him.

"Hey, Mister. Hey, Mister, why don't you go home and take a bath? You're stinky." The child giggled then skipped down the beach. In a moment Sam heard a familiar and more condemning voice.

"Hey, Mister. Why *don't* you take a bath?" Sam opened his eyes and stared at Jerry Kirbo.

"Look at you," Jerry turned up his nose. "You are putrid." Sam listened but said nothing.

"Do you think Brittany would be proud of you now? Are you just going to roll over and let her die for nothing?"

"Go fuck yourself," said Sam. He turned over and closed his eyes.

"You know what, Sam?" Jerry eyed him gravely. "I'd rid the world of you but you're not worth killing."

"Don't do me any favors." Sam lay motionless, his back toward Jerry.

"I don't want to do *you* any favors, Sam," Jerry took a step closer. "But I would like to do one for Wilton. He cares what happened to his daughter...even if you don't."

Cut to the heart, Sam rolled to his knees and tried to come to his feet as he lunged for Jerry. Jerry shoved him back with his foot, and Sam went face first into the sand. Before he could make another move, Jerry was on top of him.

"Get off me, you son of a bitch," Sam struggled hard but it was futile.

"If you care so much why don't you get up and fight for her?" Jerry yelled.

"Because you can't fight City Hall," Sam yelled back, his face shoved deeper into the sand. "Nobody gives a shit. Now let me up you..."

"I give a shit," Jerry shoved the back of Sam's head harder and his face went even deeper. "And I think we can beat the bastards."

"We? What are you? A fuckin' lawyer," Sam bellowed.

"Yeah. As a matter of fact, I am," Jerry yelled back.

There was silence. When Sam eased his struggle, Jerry softened his hold. After a moment, he released Sam, then came to his feet. He reached into his pocket and dropped a hundred dollar bill to the sand.

"There. Go buy some clothes and get your ass to my boat. Get cleaned up and find something to eat."

Sam's eyes looked empty, devoid of hope. Jerry didn't know if he was even listening.

"Get off your ass! Do you hear me?" Sam just sat and stared at the water.

Jerry removed his rose colored-glasses and assailed Sam once more. His eyes were deep blue and radiated his determination. He grabbed hard at Sam's shoulder and shook it. He looked toward the figurine that lay in the sand beside the urn and yelled, *"I said, do you hear me? Do you think Brittany is proud of you now?"*

Sam sat un-moved by the soliloquy. Jerry

slapped him on the back of his head then pointed toward the figurine. "And a little Brasso will clean that right up!"

Jerry slapped him again and Sam did nothing.

"Get up," Jerry yelled. "Get up, you drunken piece of shit," said Jerry. Finally, Jerry wiped the sand from his hands and walked away.

Sam sat a long while with his face in his hands. The pounding in his head, like Viking drums, was relentless. He looked at the urn, then at the hundred dollar bill. A sudden wind lifted the bill from the sand and twirled it in the air. When Sam grabbed for it, the pain between his temples jolted to the back of his head and his eyes closed as he caught the money.

His guts boiled and he heaved uncontrollably. He heaved again but it produced nothing. He held his stomach in his arms and tried to calm the convulsions.

"I gotta have a drink," Sam choked.

He rolled to his knees and little by little he managed to stand. The world spun wildly as he fought to keep his balance. When he bent over to pick up the urn and the statue, the blinding pain shot through his head again.

Sam took his bearings, then climbed over

the dunes and made his way to Butler Ave. He stumbled up the highway until he reached city hall where his car was parked by a meter. The battered Mustang was evidence of a man with one foot in the abyss and the other on a banana peel. More than once in recent weeks Sam had wrecked his car. And more than once he'd slept it off on the cold gray cots of the Tybee Jail.

Sam fumbled with his keys to unlock the car door. Once inside he placed the urn and the statue on the passenger seat then hung his head on the steering wheel. If I can just make it to the liquor store I'll fix everything, thought Sam.

He cranked the engine and shifted into gear. When he'd parked the car the day before he'd left three wheels on the highway and one on the sidewalk. When Sam let off the clutch and the tire came off the curb, the impact sent another wave of agony through his skull.

When Sam walked into the package shop the clerk looked at him with contempt. She'd observed his slow and steady fall to the bottom of the heap. What a waste, she thought. What a total waste.

Sam brought three half gallon bottles of whiskey to the register and held out the hundred dollar bill. Three bottles ought to kill the pain, Sam thought. When he looked behind the counter and into the mirror, his eyes flashed at the sight.

It was *Brit*. She was standing behind him. She looked upon Sam with tears in her eyes and sorrow in her heart. Sam blinked and shook his head then looked into the mirror again. This time the apparition was gone. This time he saw himself. He saw what he'd become and it sickened him.

"My God," whispered Sam. "What have I done?"

51

Sam drove to the thrift shop to try and find something to wear. The shop was attached to a red brick building near the Catholic church. Sam was ashamed at his appearance and how he must have smelled but the woman who ran the shop offered no condemnation. Her smile seemed compassionate if not understanding.

Sam found an old pair of jeans and a white sweat shirt embossed with the DeSoto Beach Motel logo. He made his purchase then walked back to his car. As he drove toward Lazaretto Creek he thought of Mister Willie.

After arriving at Jerry's boat, Sam showered then dressed and made a pot of coffee. He poured himself a cup then walked back to his car. He cranked the engine, drove out of the marina, and turned left onto the highway. He headed toward a modest old neighborhood just off of Wheaton Street in downtown Savannah.

Since Sam was a small boy Mister Willie had always been there for him. He taught Sam to play checkers and Jack-straws. He taught him to play mumblety-peg. He taught him courage and how to stand tall and fend off the bullies. He taught him to swim and to fish and to hunt and to feed himself.

Every morning Mister Willie would get up and read the Holy Bible. When Sam was in his care he'd recite passages of scripture aloud and Sam would listen. He taught Sam reverence and how to live and how to be and how to treat people. He taught him humility and love of God and love of fellow man. He was Sam's guide in all things spiritual.

Now, Sam needed Mister Willie more than ever. Sam always tried to be a good man. He tried to do what was right. He loved his God. He tried to love his fellow man though doing so was sometimes a tall order. So why would God take Brit from him? What had he done to deserve it? What had *she* done to deserve it? Why did she have to die?

Sam parked beside a small blue row house and killed the engine. The house had a large front porch with white columns, a porch swing, and lots of green plants growing in clay pots. The porch felt cool and a nice breeze was blowing.

As Sam walked to the door he smelled the pungent odor of mustard greens and smoke from the old wood stove where the greens were simmering. When he heard Mahalia Jackson's Gospel voice coming over the stereo speakers he smiled. He knew Mister Willie was home.

Before Sam could knock he saw Mister Willie shuffling down the hall. Mister Willie smiled as he flipped the hook from the eye then opened his screen door.

"Come on in Sam. I knew you'd be comin' round one day."

Willie and Sam never called each other Mister when they weren't on the job. They were at home, and in the best of ways, they were almost family.

Willie lived with his sister Mattie and her son Kareem. When his wife died years before, he moved from Macon to Savannah to be with Mattie and to help her with her son. Mattie always said that cleanliness was next to Godliness and their home reflected her belief.

Sam followed Willie down the long linoleum hallway, past Kareem's room, past the telephone table, past all the family pictures in brass frames that hung on the wall, and finally to the kitchen. Mattie was standing at the sink washing dishes when Willie and Sam entered the room. Mattie turned and a welcome smile came to her face. She held out her arms and walked Sam's way.

"It's good to see you, little Sammy," Mattie said as she held him. "I want to thank you for what you done for Tyrone," Mattie never seemed to acknowledge that "little Sammy" was all grown up. But Sam didn't mind. Maybe it made her feel young, he thought.

Mattie was a tall woman with an imposing stature. Her hair was gray and she wore it naturally. It resembled fleece and shone around her stern, brown face like a halo. Years of work and worry had taken its toll, but since her son had turned his life around, there was always a song in her heart.

"You look like death warmed over. I bet you bout to starve to death," she said. "Now, sit down and lemme fix you a plate."

Sam knew better than to argue with her. Besides, she was right. Sam hadn't tasted Mattie's good cooking since she'd worked for his grandmother as a maid and cook thirty years previous. That was far too long, Sam thought.

Mattie loaded the plate with a helping of rice smothered with northern beans and fat back. She placed a big slice of cornbread beside the beans and spooned up a good mess of mustard greens next to that. She poured Sam a mason jar full of sweet iced tea with a slice of lemon and a sprig of peppermint then set everything down on the table.

"Now clean your plate, little Sammy," she said as she wiped her hands on her apron.

Sam picked up a bottle of pepper sauce and sprinkled it generously over the greens. Cleaning his plate would be easy. And the food was good to the last bite.

After eating, Sam and Willie went back to the front porch. Sam sat in the swing and Willie sat beside the table in an old wicker rocking chair. Willie rocked back, closed his eyes, and took a deep breath.

"What's on your mind, Sam," Willie reached into an aging King Edward cigar box and found his pipe. He opened a plastic bag and pinched a wad of tobacco between his thumb and his first two fingers. He packed the tobacco into the bowl and picked up his lighter. He listened as Sam asked for insight into the mind of God and why He had taken Brit away.

Willie groaned and puffed away at his pipe while he lit the tobacco. He leaned back again and blew the smoke up and away. He rubbed his chin and his eyes sparkled as the answer came to him.

"Lot o peoples died in dat fire," said Willie. "If sump'm ain't done, lot mo gone die," Willie cocked his head and took another puff.

Willie told Sam that Brit was in a far better place than this old world. And the Good Book says, the eye has not seen nor has the ear heard of the things the Lord has prepared for those who love Him. He told Sam that his separation from Brit was only for a time. And the Book says, we know that all things work together for good to them that love God, to them who are called according to His purpose.

And maybe it took the loss of the most beautiful flower He'd created to spur Sam into action and make him serve that purpose. Willie said because of Brit's death, Sam must take up his sword, fight the good fight, and make a difference. "Sometime," said Willie. "Da Lord have to take da very best."

A new sense of understanding transcended Sam as his fate came before him. He was given the courage to bear the unbearable, and the power to do battle.

52

By early evening Sam's head had cleared completely and the seltzer had calmed his stomach. He sat at the little table on Jerry's boat and polished the figurine with liquid brass cleaner and a soft cloth. Brit had always displayed the piece on the mantle and she'd always kept it shining.

It was six o'clock before Jerry returned. He was dressed in a business suit and he carried a stack of law books. He was pleasantly surprised to find that Sam had come around.

"It must have taken a miracle to bring you to your senses," said Jerry.

"It did," said Sam, with an expression of resolve.

"I'm glad you're looking better," Jerry said, opening his brief case. "There's much to do so let's get after it."

Sam and Jerry sat until nearly eleven P.M. formulating a plan of action. The following morning Jerry went to the courthouse and filed suit on Sam's behalf. The court system was backed up and it would be some time before the case would come on the docket. The suit alleged that Chatham County and the City of Tybee Island were negligent, both in their in-

spection procedures, and the administration of
State law, which directly resulted in the pain,
suffering, and death of Brittany Veronica Lewis.

Jerry was still a mystery. Sam didn't know
his chances of slaying the dragon that killed his
wife but one thing was sure, if anyone could
don the breastplate of rectitude, gird his loins
with truth, and lead the charge, it was Jerry
Kirbo.

For the next few months, Jerry and Sam
worked diligently. Each law the city and county
ignored was examined to the last letter. Every
code violation broken was scrutinized to the final degree.

Jerry Kirbo was as good as the best before he retired. Tort had been his field. Once in
a blue moon Jerry would come out of retire-
ment to champion a cause that impassioned
him. And no cause he'd championed ever fueled him so fiercely.

He was living proof the term good lawyer
wasn't a contradiction of itself. In all his years
of practice he never once took a case he didn't
believe in. And he never declined a case he believed in when he knew the odds were stacked
against him and his client couldn't pay. He won
more than he lost, and the ideals he held in
college followed him when he passed the Bar

and hung out his sign.

After a long period of discovery Sam had his day in court. Ten days into the litigation, just before the jury retired for deliberation, the Superior Court judge spoke to the court. The Honorable Albert Baker subtly reminded the jurors to disregard that any award they might find for Sam would be taken from the county's and the City of Tybee's general funds and given at the tax-payer's expense.

Justice was usually there for those who could afford it and Wilton picked up the tab. Still, there was the threat of higher taxes. That notion weighed heavily on the minds of the twelve honest men and women who made up the jury. Fighting City Hall weighed heavily on Sam's.

Jerry believed the preponderance of evidence was in Sam's favor. He also believed that the chances of those good citizens sitting in the jury box and voting themselves a tax increase was questionable. After ten days away from their usual routines, they were restless and ready to get on with their lives. The smidgen of money they were paid every day did little to bolster their enthusiasm.

Although the core of the case was Brit's wrongful death and the allegation that her death was directly caused by the county's and the City of Tybee's negligence, the scope was broader. Submitted into evidence were the State of Georgia Construction Industry Licensing Board Acts, Rules, and Regulations. Since Sam's expertise was primarily in the plumbing field, so too was that dimension of the case. First, the primary terms examined were defined for the jurors:

During the proceedings it was shown that only persons licensed by the Sate Of Georgia were permitted to perform plumbing work within the state. The only exemptions provided by Georgia Laws O.C.G.A. 43-14-2 (9), (10), (11), and (12) were for employees working in public service positions such as for gas companies, electrical service providers, or water departments. Exceptions were also provided for agricultural workers, in some instances, regarding irrigation.

Personnel working for county or city municipalities were also exempt from the law. Still the exemptions pertained strictly to employees working at their jobs. The law did not prohibit individuals from performing plumbing in their personal dwellings as long as the work was in compliance with the code.

It was established that the county and the City of Tybee Island were derelict in their duty to enforce state law and see that only licensed plumbers were permitted to install plumbing and every construction job was manned by a minimum of a journeyman plumber. Evidence further showed the lack of regard for the laws of the State of Georgia was not only deliberate, but blatant.

It was shown that the provision for allowing individuals to plumb their own residences if the work complied with the code was ludicrous. How could the county see that the work was in compliance with the code when they sent out inspectors like Ms. Holmes who didn't know a soil stack from a wet vent?

In depositions prior to the case coming before the court, and also during testimony, all county inspectors stated they were not told by Jim Hoffmeyer, the county Director of Inspections, nor the City of Tybee Island to require complicity with the law. When cross-examined, Mister Hoffmeyer stated that, if he followed the law and did as prescribed, the giant machine of progress would grind to a halt because there were precious few licensed journeymen plumbers in the area.

Jerry Kirbo asked the director if that same rule of reason should prevail if heart surgeons were in short supply. Perhaps the director would

like to take a ride in an airplane with an unlicensed pilot who didn't know an altimeter from
a pitot tube, Jerry suggested. Or how about
letting Sam perform a little general dentistry on
him? Sam had a chisel, a hammerdrill and a
big set of pliers.

There was murmuring and laughter in the
courtroom. The judge banged his gavel and
demanded order. He banged again and threatened to clear the room. Quickly, the noise subsided.

Much time was given to the lack of professionalism regarding the other trades as well.
Jerry showed that unqualified tradesmen who
lacked the skill, the knowledge, and the license
to perform tasks that should have been reserved
for the competent, were allowed unchecked, to
peddle their sub-skills to the detriment and at
the expense of the public at large.

Later during the proceedings Jerry submitted exhibit 37, a classified advertisement
printed in a weekly newspaper. The add offered
the services of "Handy Andy, the Dandy Handy-
man, jack of all trades." For half the price of
the big guys with the high overhead, Handy Andy
could see to all one's household needs. Andy
could paint, build that deck, roof a house, mend
a fence, and fix a pesky electrical outlet that

didn't always work. He could stop a drippy faucet and he was running a special that week. For twenty bucks, Andy would clean your air ducts and make sure your compressor was "hummin' like a bumble bee."

The county regularly permitted unlicensed individuals to advertise their services. The practice was illegal, it was dangerous, and it was a slap in the face to legitimate craftsmen. It was shown that people had lost their possessions, their homes, even their lives by trusting the likes of Handy Andy. And "jack of all trades" was always properly followed by "and master of none."

The jury had been in deliberation just over an hour before reaching their decision. Sam and Jerry were standing by the monument housing the eternal flame beneath the halls of justice when the bailiff came walking their way.

"Looks like this is it," Sam said as he wiped the sweat from his forehead.

"Yes it is, Sam," Jerry sighed. "They've either found for us or they've found for the devil."

53

Sam looked out the window of the Quantas air liner as the giant 747 descended from 30,000 feet above the Pacific Ocean. He felt a strange kinship with the land where destiny would soon find him. The airplane touched down in Brisbane just before three o'clock that after-noon.

As the plane taxied off the runway Sam's mood was somber. He thought of battles won and of battles lost. He'd been told he'd won the war but there was no celebration. And the spoils of victory brought no joy. Mostly Sam thought of Brit.

Sam was awarded a million dollars for the wrongful death of his soul mate. And he was given twenty-six million more for punitive dam-ages.

Legislation had been proposed to mandate that all who offered their services as a builder or a general contractor be duly licensed by the state. During the discovery period of the litiga-tion, Sam learned the state had lowered its stan-dards by issuing limited licenses to those who lacked the knowledge or ability to stand the examination required to become a true Master. Sam also learned the dumbing down included the policy of open book testing. Attached to the legislation was a rider abolishing those policies.

Sam set aside enough money to pay his salary and keep him through his old age. The rest he invested and formed a trust to finance a watchdog group of professionals. Masters of their respective trades would perform exhaustive inspections on all renovations and new construction within Chatham county, and throughout the State of Georgia.

Sam's job would be to oversee the inspectors and to direct funding and operations of the non-prophet, philanthropic organization. The trust would be called the Brittany Veronica Lewis Memorial Fund. Sam would waste no time returning to America and to Tybee Island. He would carry the banner of excellence and bear the torch of accountability.

Wilton Hayes stood watching as the plane pulled into the terminal. Soon, the passengers began pouring into the waiting area as Wilton scanned the crowd. There were 261 passengers on board the airliner that day. After a few moments, Wilton spotted Sam in the crowd.

There was no bounce in Sam's step, no pep in his stride, when he walked down the portable corridor and into the room. He managed a smile when Wilton greeted him, but his eyes were the windows to his woe. His countenance had changed, his expression, an empty one. His movements were those of an automaton: lifeless, yet with definiteness of purpose.

"I've made the arrangements, Sam'o," Wilton said with respect. "The pilot is here; the plane is fueled and waiting."

"I want you to go with me," Sam said as they walked to the baggage claim area.

"I don't know if I can bear it," Wilton's lip trembled. "Are you sure that's what you want?"

Sam hesitated a moment, then said, "Brit would have wanted it that way."

The bush-pilot loaded Sam's suitcase into the baggage compartment of the twin engine Piper Seneca, then the three boarded the plane. In less than an hour, the airplane was approaching a private landing strip on Fraser Island, just five kilometers south of the Great Sandy National Park. Sam observed the pilots skill as he turned left from the base leg onto his final approach. The runway was short but the pilot took his business in stride.

As the plane taxied off the end of the grassy landing strip, Wilton pointed to a four-wheel drive vehicle that looked like a military personnel carrier. The Jeep-like transport sat high off the ground on nobby tires and was painted as for desert camouflage.

"That'll take us where we need to go," Wilton said to Sam.

"How far is it?" Sam asked, feeling like a

pilgrim, traveling to the edge of the world.

"It's only twenty-five kilometers due north," Wilton told him. "But some of the bush is fairly rough between here and there. It'll take nearly an hour and a half."

Standing next to the vehicle was the old one, Eloi Unaipon. As Sam and Wilton approached the vehicle, Eloi greeted them with a simple nod. He opened the door and they climbed into the back seat. Sam placed his suitcase behind him in the bed of the vehicle then watched as Eloi shut the door and walked around to the other side. He stepped up into the seat, started the engine, and the vehicle moved forward out of the field and into the bush.

The journey would have been thrilling if circumstances had been different. Fraser Island was exactly as Brit described. It was 125 kilometers long and 160,000 hectares in area, which made it the world's largest sand island.

The dune systems of the Great Sandy Region, which included Fraser Island, were some of the oldest and largest on the planet. Many dunes were over 200 meters in height. At times they took on sculptured shapes which earned them such names as "The Cathedrals" and "The Pinnacles." There were seventy-two different colored sands found on the island. The sands on the thirty-five kilometer stretch of beach north of Happy Valley were the most vividly colored.

Inland from Happy Valley and further north, the Yidney Scrub, was home to a 200 year-old forest of kauri pines. The western coastline was fringed with mangroves, vast areas of cypress, and sandy beaches with crystal clear creeks and streams running through them into the sheltered waters of Hervey Bay.

Fraser Island was home to more than 200 species of birds as well as a variety of amphibians, snakes and other reptiles. An array of animals, including wallabies, flying foxes, and opossums roamed the land. The route the three followed that afternoon took them, not only through beautiful rain forests but also through heathlands where shrubs, scribbly gum trees and wallum banksia flourished. It was late November, spring down under, and the scent of a profusion of wildflowers filled the air.

Precisely an hour and a half after the last leg of Sam's journey began, the all-terrain vehicle came to rest on an endless sandy beach, bordering placid waters. Sam came out of his seat and around the back of the vehicle. He zipped open his suitcase and removed the silver urn with the message, God Is Love.

He walked back around the vehicle and held the urn for Wilton and Eloi to see. Giving up any notion of holding back his tears, Wilton stroked the urn with the back of his fingers. After a few moments, Sam spoke.

"It's time, Wilton."

"Yes, son," said Wilton, his voice unsteady. "It is indeed time."

Sam walked to the water's edge and removed his shoes. The sand was warm and it was dry. He turned northeast and followed the deserted shoreline a long while until he came to the place Brit had told him of. It was the place of their "Dreaming." Sam sat on the sand, cradled the urn in his arms, and he waited.

The earth turned and twilight's mysterious glow replaced the fiery sunset. From the distance came the unearthly resonance of a tribesman's didgeridoo telling the story of all creation. The earth, the sun, and the planets did as they'd done from the beginning. In perfect design the bodies of the cosmos spinned and tumbled at the whim of the Creator.

In the beginning God created the heaven and the earth. And the earth was without form, and void; and darkness was upon the face of the deep. And the Spirit of God moved upon the face of the waters. In the beginning was the

Word, and the Word was with God, and the Word was God. The same was in the beginning with God. All things were made by Him; and without Him was not anything made that was made.

The Aborigine believed that, in the Dreamtime, the Creation Ancestors roamed the void before giving birth to life. They created physical features of the earth: the Cathedrals and the Pinnacles and the mountains and the valleys. Then they created the animals and the birds and the fish and the people. When they were finished, the Ancestors absorbed themselves into their own creation. Powerful Dreaming sites were created where the Ancestors were absorbed.

Sam sat with the urn on the sand near the most powerful site of all. He waited in darkness and looked to the west for a sign. As time grew near he was absorbed into the Dreaming. The didgeridoo's haunting vibration filled the Cathedral as the huge full moon rose from behind Sam and high over the still waters of Platypus Bay.

As the moon descended the western sky, tiny bubbles of sea foam twinkled on the shore, where the path of light leading to the mysterious golden moon began its quest. Then there was quiet and Sam felt the power. Here was a

time that lived in his heart. Here was a time for
a promise kept.

Sam removed his clothing and dropped it
to the sand. He caressed the urn and slowly
followed the path into the water. A warm sensation overtook him as Brit drew near. When
waist deep in the water, he opened the urn and
held it high above his head. When shoulder
deep, with reverence and devotion, he poured
her ashes.

When they filtered into the pristine water,
the ashes assumed a golden glow. As they flickered and glittered and bathed in moonlight, they
drifted toward Sam and they clinged to his body.

Sam closed his eyes, turned his face to the
heavens, and basked in her presence. Her eyes
glistened with joyous tears while her palms
found his face. Softly, she kissed his lips, then
whispered,

"My love,
How long I have waited for your gentle touch
The smile in your eyes that I love so much
The warmth of your body once more
one with mine
The song in your voice again so sublime
Platypus Bay...Platypus Bay
The angels all come here to kneel and to pray
Platypus Bay...Platypus Bay

They trouble the waters for healing they say
Platypus Bay...Platypus Bay
Let us be one in eternity's play
Platypus Bay...Platypus Bay
Our souls will be cleansed
then we'll fly away."

There he lingered. He felt wind on his face then heard a rushing. He opened his eyes and three white doves fluttered round about him. As suddenly as they came, the doves were gone. Sam looked into the water, and so too were Brit's ashes, gone with the tide.

The End

The following are excerpts from a report made
by the
Department Of The Treasury
Bureau of Alcohol, Tobacco, and Firearms
The report was obtained by virtue of the
Freedom of Information Act (FOIA)

Investigation number 113360-95-0048 D
FIRE ORIGIN AND CAUSE REPORT
February 10, 1995
Yarbrough Residence
1205 Sand Point Run
Tybee Island, Georgia:

SYNOPSIS OF THE INCIDENT
Page 1, paragraph 1

"On February 5, 1995, at 0459 hours the
Tybee Island Volunteer Fire Department was
notified of a fire at 1205 Sand Point Run, Tybee
Island, Georgia. Responding police officers
found the three-story wood home fully involved
in flames. The first firetruck responded within
nine minutes. Firefighters observed flames vent-
ing through the roof of the kitchen in a diam-
eter of about twelve feet. The kitchen and living
area were fully involved in fire, with flames
spreading to the third floor. A sixteen year old
jumped from her second floor bedroom deck,
but her mother perished in the fire in the third

floor bedroom. High northwesterly winds fanned the flames, but firefighters extinguished the blaze before the third and second floor structures were destroyed"

Page 4, paragraphs 6, 7 & 8

"An east/west floor joist immediately adjacent to the south of the studded kitchen half wall was burned in half. The pattern of char indicated that the fire originated to the south of this joist. Three east/west floor joists had been completely burned from at a distance of about two feet from the studded wall to the kitchen.

"Examination of the floor joists and flooring in this area indicated that the fire originated between the floor joists, above the plywood garage ceiling and below the wood floor to the dining area. The area was located adjacent to the east wall around the sliding glass door entrance area to the dining room.

"Several insulated copper wires ran parallel to the easternmost north/south floor joist, and had been affixed to the joist by metal braids or staples. The wires had burned in two in the area of origin - just north of the sliding glass door - and indications of arcing were observed to the separated ends."

Page 5

CONCLUSION

"Firefighters concluded that the cause of the fire is accidental. A smoldering fire developed in the floor joists on the east wall by heat generated by an electrical malfunction. The fire evolved into a free burning state over time and spread to the upper floors of the structure."

Fatalities/Injuries

"Teresa Yarbrough, 39 years of age, died from the inhalation of hot gases and heat exposure."

Estimated Value of Loss

"The loss is estimated to be in excess of $136,000."

Afterword

Was the fire that caused Teresa Yarbrough's death an accident, as the A.T.F. report stated, or was it due to an act of incompetence? There *is* a difference, I think. But the investigation is closed so we may never know. Was Teresa Yarbrough's life worth more than $136,000.00? Yes it was. But the value of a human life can't be measured that way. Can it?

Based on my experience of twenty-seven years in the construction industry, I state the following with authority and conviction: All general contractors doing business in the State of Georgia should be licensed by the state and required to stand an examination on the minimum building codes of Georgia and the Southern Building Code. Those individuals currently engaged in the general contracting business should be given a reasonable time to prepare for the exam and a "grandfather clause" exempting them from examination should not apply.

Similarly, legislation should be written mandating that all building inspectors be experts in the trades they are inspecting. Furthermore, the Inspection Departments of all counties and municipalities should be held liable for failure to enforce the codes.

I urge all who read this book to contact their legislators and require accountability from those engaged in the building business and from those who inspect them. Require professionalism or expect the inferior. Demand excellence or court disaster. The life you save may be your own.

Billy Doniel

About the Author

Billy Doniel was born in 1953 at Robins Air Force Base, Georgia. He grew up in Macon where he attended Macon Junior College and Mercer University. He moved his residence to Savannah in 1985.

He has held a real estate license in the state of Georgia and a Master plumber's license in the state of Maine. He is a private pilot, rescue diver, and accomplished underwater hunter. He currently holds a non-restricted Master plumber's license in the state of Georgia.

Billy lives on Tybee Island with his wife, Veronica, and their boy, Clyde, the English Mastiff. Woof!